South Beulah, Minnesota

About the Cover
Conte drawing, "Jigging Duffer"
by David Staff (1937-1976)

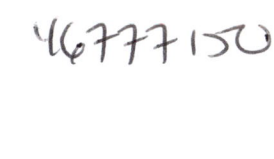

South Beulah, Minnesota

short stories
Harold Huber

Stone House Press, Inc.
2000

© 2000 Harold Huber

First printing, July 2000

All rights reserved under International and Pan-American Copyright Conventions. No part of this book may be reproduced or transmitted in any form or by any means, electronic, mechanical, including photocopying, recording, or by any information storage and retrieval system, except in the case of reviews, without the express written permission of the copyright holder and/or publisher, except where permitted by law.

This is a work of fiction. Any resemblance of the characters herein to real life or deceased persons is only coincidental.

Cover drawing, "Jigging Duffer," by David Staff
Cover design by Jane Geisinger

ISBN Number: 0-9675060-0-x
Library of Congress Card Number: 00-103727

Published by Stone House Press, Inc.
Richville MN 56576

Printed in Canada

*Special thanks
to my special muses,
Carole and Jannie,
and to my crafty accomplices,
Jolie and Jim
for guiding me through
this gallery of old duffers
and young scalawags.*

Several stories from
South Beulah, Minnesota
were previously published in the following
literary journals and periodicals:

"Emancipation in B-Flat" in *Satire*
"Caroline's Snake" and "The Twins" in *Sweet Annie Press*
"Catching Up" and "The Pinky Quest" in *Medicinal Purpose*
"Gerald and Juliet" in *New Jersey Review*
"Willy's Fall" in *Pearl*
"The Twenty-Fifth Circle" in *River Images*
"Blood Brothers" in *Dan River Anthology*
"Polly's Dance" in *Loonfeather Press*
"Letter To Charles" in *Fall Creek Press*

This book is funded in part by a grant from the
Lake Region Arts Council through a
Minnesota State Legislative appropriation.

Contents

Emancipation in B-Flat 1
A Heart for Gypsy Lily 7
Caroline's Snake 17
A Cowboy's Sweetheart 25
The Twins 33
Chapter Three 41
The Grapes of St. Billy 49
Look-to Love Song 59
Catching Up 65
Gerald and Juliet 71
The Pinky Quest 77
Willy's Fall 83
The Twenty-Fifth Circle 87
Blood Brothers 95
Polly's Dance 101
Letter To Charles 111

South Beulah, Minnesota

Emancipation in B-Flat

1985

Although none but she possessed the skill to perform her music, and despite being known to only a handful of contemporaries, the fact remained that Bernadette was a mighty composer. The human voice was her instrument and her entire opus output was designed for it. The sun seldom completed its journey from the spire of South Beulah State Bank to the smoke stacks of Euclid Tannery without having witnessed the creation of several major works. Wagner and Strauss lived again in Bernadette, in that words and music held equal rank in each piece. Her masterpiece of the morning was, "I Hate Everybody—Everybody Stinks."

Rossini might also be mentioned in connection with her work, since florid passages were important and ever-present ingredients. When singing the word "stii-iii-iii-inks," for example, the rocket-launch ferocity of her coloratura, the bewildering complexities of her vocal patterns, and the almost supernatural duration of her stratospheric flights, brought all listeners—even neighborhood dogs—to a paralytic standstill. She composed for her own aesthetic fulfillment, but she *performed* with certain sociological goals in mind. The foremost of which was the art of Absolute Dominion... over her parents, neighbors and playfellows.

The power of her music helped immeasurably in this quest, but it was the unwitting legacy from each parent that all but guaranteed success. From her mother, who *was* Evangeline's Beauty Emporium, Bernadette learned that color was a tremendous aid in swaying men's minds. Fearless application of cosmetics (pilfered from Mother's stock) to the bangs-framed square of her face usually resulted in a living mask, half German Expressionism, half Viking masthead.

From her father, who wrestled semi-professionally under the name of "The Foul Marauder," Bernadette inherited both stance and gait. Therefore, her lyrical gifts aside, the very design and impact of her visage struck terror into the hearts of standard children. They would gladly have avoided her company, but Bernadette was ruthless in searching them out.

All classic games of childhood were reinterpreted and tailored to her needs. As an example, Bernadette's rule for hide-and-seek was: Bernadette hides, everyone else seeks—and nobody finds. All in all, she gave new meaning to the words, "Suffer the little children."

This great musical career began two years earlier, when Bernadette was nine years old. A regional troupe had performed "Hansel and Gretel" at her school, and while the message of the opera escaped her notice, the idiom was clasped to her muscular little bosom. From that day, most communicating between Bernadette and her play-victims was done in song. After a chance viewing of the Salome/John-the-Baptist scene on a PBS program one evening, Bernadette's quaking subjects lived in dread of the pronouncement: "We're going to play *beheading.*" For so many on and around Euclid Avenue, the days of childhood were interminable, indeed.

On the morning of "I Hate Everybody—Everybody Stinks," there was a new kind of tension in the air, for those producers of stink, as well as for the young hatress. A gargantuan moving van was parked in front of the house next door. With adult faces peering out of windows, and with a line of youngsters held in rigid check behind the outstretched arms of Herodias's daughter, all watched the comings and goings of the moving men. While grown-up eyes judged the taste and quality of the newcomer's possessions, Bernadette's were checking for signs of the owner's progeny—on special alert for clues indicating gender. As soon as she had determined there were two adults and a *male* offspring, she rubbed her hands in anticipation and led her troops to the nearby dump for another session of decapitation. That night, her

Emancipation in B-Flat

dream was a slightly distorted version of the Judith-Holofernes legend.

When morning came, Bernadette applied a particularly gaudy layer of facial decor, then ran to her waiting station behind a garbage can. The target was already bustling with activity, but, as yet, no sign of *him*. After what seemed a month of hours, the movers drove away and an eerie silence descended on the scene. Shifting her crouched position and chewing her lipstick, Bernadette maintained a vigil, feeling deep within herself that a silver-platter moment was at hand.

In what seemed cinematic slow motion, a slender, tow-headed boy emerged from the house. Bernadette rose to her full height. The fragile looking lad wandered aimlessly around his new yard, gracefully brushing a hand or foot over objects scattered there. Bernadette loosened her jumper straps for greater freedom of movement. He picked a dandelion and, with meticulous care, tucked it in the buttonhole of his shirt. The watcher did four fast push-ups. When the boy's ambling footsteps aimed at their adjoining property line, Bernadette swaggered into his path.

Radiant with innocence, the gentle-stepping newcomer smiled sweetly and walked toward his new neighbor. Bernadette bore down, mentally pumping iron. From shy, pink lips, a quiet "hullo" issued forth. Then, with no further word, he turned and strolled to the front sidewalk. The bewildered amazon froze—stunned by the stinging insult of lack-of-fascination-and-fear. Her cosmetic colors changed values because of the burning red that now underlay them. The earth shook as she charged to the sidewalk, passed the boy, then turned to confront him. With fists fused to hips, her usual rectangularity was transformed into an ominous hexagon.

"What's your name?" Bernadette demanded.
"Frederick," was the lad's delicate reply.
"Mine's Bernadette, but nobody calls me that… and lives."
"What should I call you?" he asked meekly.
"Terminator!"
"That's not a girl's name, is it?" he civilly inquired.
"That's what you'll call me, Freddy Boy."
"My name is Frederick."

"Yeah? From now on, your name is 'Nerd-Face'... got that?"

In less time than it takes a pearl to drop to the bottom of a glass of wine, a fist plowed into Bernadette's mid-section. With bangs crissing and crossing, and with lips protruded in an exhaling "oooo," she found herself keester-sprawled on the cruel cement. In a rare moment of strategic miscalculation, she lifted her eyes to the enemy before deciding on the appropriate facial expression. Frederick, no mean strategist himself, looked down through the Revlon glaze, and, seeing there a face caught in neutral, smiled and once more said, "My name is Frederick." Then, stooping low so that one golden lock lay bangs-entwined with black, he added, "*Got that?*"

A long pause ensued, during which Bernadette's right and left brain lobes engaged in civil war. Finally, in a flattened mezza-voice, she answered, "Got it."

An angel's expression underlined an angelic tone as the boy asked, "Would you like to see my aquarium?" Witnessing this unheard of, undemonstrative brand of physical prowess, combined with her ungovernable lust for captive wildlife caused her to choose "peaceful coexistence" as the plan of the moment. Frederick put his arm across her shoulder as they walked to his house. Tense, nail-biting observers dropped their hands in astonishment when they saw this pale, freckled band of arm resting calmly on the massive meat of Bernadette's head-holder.

An hour later, they were side by side on their knees in the grass.

"You ever heard of Catherine the Great?" the television-wise girl asked.

"Oh yes," he answered, "Have you ever heard of Frederick the Great?"

She hadn't, but recognizing the regal ring in the title, she claimed the knowledge as her own. After these designations were formally *"I Declare You"*-ed, their conversation turned to more practical matters.

"Do you want to get married?" Frederick asked.

"Sure," she responded without hesitation.

"Okay," the boy said, "but let's not tell our parents."

Emancipation in B-Flat

In her final act as an unmarried despot, Bernadette ferreted out a dozen of her quaking underlings and organized the most brilliant wedding her parents' two-car garage had ever held. She officiated as both priestess and coloratura soloist. She extemporaneously composed and performed a *GRAND CANTATA FOR SOLO BRIDE* titled, "Oh Frederick and Catherine, They Are So Great—And Everybody Else Stinks." As she sustained an incredible final top note, Frederick lifted his slender voice an octave higher in a shimmering "I do." With that, and the customary required applause, the nuptial jubilee ended.

For the remainder of the summer, the newlyweds were inseparable. Occasional attempts on the wife's part to take her man unawares and regain sole dominion were always thwarted by the husband's unexpected maneuvers. Bernadette's makeup became more subtle and refined, and her musical output changed dramatically. Vengeance arias and mad scenes were gradually replaced with cowboy songs and, much to the surprise of concealed listeners, sentimental ballads. While Frederick instructed Bernadette in the splendors of mind-over-brawn, she taught him many of the finer points of vocal production and ruthless cunning.

After nearly a week of peering out from concealed hiding places, the neighborhood children mutually concluded that the erstwhile Princess of Judea no longer considered them to be of interest or value, and they experienced the sublime joy of emancipation. Ropes were swung and jumpers once again took turns. Dolls were taken for peaceful rides in coaster wagons. Hide-and-seek was played by the old rules. Soon, worry-lines faded from adult brows. Both parents and offspring took comfort in knowing that, henceforth, all things operatic would be confined to those untouched channels on their television sets, and that the darkest period of their lives was now history.

South Beulah, Minnesota   Harold Huber

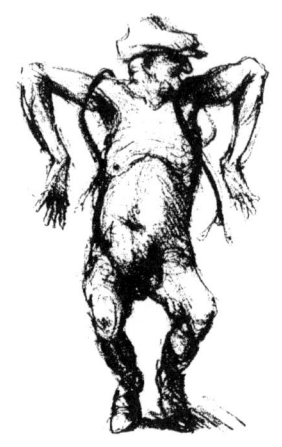

A Heart for Gypsy Lily

1970

They were shoe prints, anybody could see that, but why did they look so queer? A collar of snow was raised at the front of each track as though some dragging weight had been suddenly yanked into the air. Andrew paraded all known draggables across his mind, but none proved satisfactory. The crows? He wouldn't put it past them! If one sat in the middle of each print and slid on its stomach and pushed with its... No, the birds had just landed when the school bus pulled up to his house, and they flapped away the second he jumped off.

A black shape came into view at the end of the block. It paused, then began floating in the boy's direction. As it slid closer, Andrew saw that it was an old woman. He sat on one of the broad brick ledges flanking the house steps. His thighs rhythmically squeezed and patted a ridge of snow between his legs while he stared at the approaching form.

She was wrapped in a heavy dark coat, a shawl hiding much of her face. Each hand was buried in an opposite sleeve and her head was dropped so low that her back hunched out like the buffalos in his nickel collection. When she had passed, the boy sprang to the sidewalk to check for prints. It was her... *she* made the tracks! As he ran to overtake the bent figure, his boots slapped a chain of craters into the fine veil of new-fallen snow.

Andrew matched his pace to the woman's and, in a small voice, said, "Hi." She continued walking, studying the whiteness in her path. The boy gazed downward too. Her feet pressed forward in a slow-motion glide. The wide toes of her galoshes plowed long trenches. It was good to have the mysterious prints explained, but the woman's silence bothered him. It felt mean, like something angry and unfair. Maybe she is deaf, Andrew thought, or maybe he hadn't actually spoken aloud, after all. He decided to try again.

"Hi. I'm Andrew. But please don't call me 'Drew' or 'Andy,' because my mother says that's cheap," he spoke in explosive tones meant to simulate adult disdain, "… but so are things that don't cost much money. Do you know what cheap means… exactly?"

The woman stopped for a moment, then trudged forward.

"Cheap and sheep," she said quietly, "they're both what people are. Weep and reap—that's what people do. Go play!"

Andrew wondered if it were the clouds of steam around her mouth that made her voice sound cracked and wavery. "I *am* playing," he protested. "Besides, there's nobody to play with yet. We just moved here one week ago. That's our house back there." Andrew turned and pointed. His finger aimed at his own bedroom window, where Batman and Robin dangled from a pullstring on the shade. After waving to his puppet friends, he spun around to make sure she was looking at the right spot. The old lady was halfway down the block.

"I know where you live," said Andrew, once again at the woman's side.

"Where?"

"Down around that corner someplace. I tried to follow your trail before, but there were too many tracks to tell for sure. I hope it's the house with the little castles on the roof." Since this topic seemed as fruitless as the others, he tried a new tack.

"You're old, aren't you?"

"Yes," was her flat reply.

"Are you one hundred?"

"Probably."

A hint of supplication narrowed the boy's voice. "I don't know any old people."

"You've got grandparents."

"Only in the pictures on the piano, and they're not nearly as old as you are."

"Oh."

Heel first, Andrew squat-walked a few steps in the woman's

A Heart for Gypsy Lily

path, thinking he could break into her lowered gaze. The effort was useless, so he moved back to her side and studied her shifting feet.

"You wear men's overshoes, don't you?"

"Yes."

"Don't you like ladies'?"

"No."

"Me neither," he concurred, planting each boot with cowboy impact.

Two crows, perched in the top branches of a naked elm, stopped their acidic complaints and looked down. They saw double stripes being drawn around their plot of rooftops and trees. Long stripes on one trail, short dashes on the other. Shortly after the trail-makers turned the corner, bird-peace was reestablished and the high air was once again filled with shrieks to distant relatives.

* * *

Batman and Robin were silhouettes against the starlit, half-open window. Andrew pushed the pillows upward with his shoulders to gain a better viewing angle. The dolls were suspended, belly-to-belly, from the shadestring. In this position, they could easily whisper secret plans during the night. Night—the time when so much *thinking* happened to a person. In former times, the nighttime darkness of his room invited a quick slide into sleep. But since moving to this new neighborhood, the black air seemed to turn his brain on. So far, his comic book heroes were his only playmates. But now that he had met the lady in overshoes, things might be different. He wondered if she were at all interested in fighting crime. He pictured the two of them making snow angels in the front yard. It was Andrew's last conscious thought.

He opened his eyes. The sunlight looked hot on the window's glass. It threw a shadow of his crime-fighters to the floor. The swaying shape reminded Andrew of something. "The Walking Lady!" he cried, lurching from the warm bedding and flailing into his clothes.

* * *

A thin layer of new snow had once more smoothed the horizontal world. Andrew inspected the crosswalk. No fresh tracks—no old ladies in sight. He practiced angel-making in the snow to pass the time. Eventually, in a space between houses at the end of the block, a bowed outline inched forward. The excited boy ran to the corner to wait. When the woman passed him and started down Andrew's street, she gave no sign of noticing him.

"Hello, lady. It's me. I waited for you."

He caught up to her, checked his gallop and copied her slow, gliding steps. Satisfied that they were perfectly synchronized, he scrutinized her solemn profile and smiled.

"You don't like to talk, do you?"

The woman shook her head.

"I do… especially when the words freeze coming out." He blew a series of sound-puffs into the air. "See? Ooo-ooo-oooooh."

"Ooo rhymes with fool," she muttered.

Andrew mimicked her scowl, then lowered his head and hunched his back, thinking she would take the imitation as a compliment and be more friendly.

"You don't like to be polite, do you?"

"No."

"People won't like you if you're not."

"Let them not."

"They won't love you anymore, either."

"Love?" The old woman stopped and raised her eyes to meet the boy's for the first time.

Andrew had never seen such eyes. They were all black, like his prize marbles, and her lids were speckly hoods with little folds in them. Her lips wrinkled when she spoke.

"You should be ashamed, using that word," she scolded.

"Don't you like love?"

"No."

"You *hate* love?" Andrew asked in disbelief.

"I am not a fool," she replied. "Wise people fear it."

"I like it," the boy said proudly.

"You don't know the meaning… who is it you love?"

"I love Henry, my best friend in Minneapolis. And my mother and my father. And God. And Batman."

A Heart for Gypsy Lily

"And you think they love you too?"

"They *do*!" Andrew shouted. "All kinds of people do. I got cards from everybody at my new school—a whole handful—over a thousand! And it isn't even Valentine's Day until Sunday. I even got one in the mailbox, from Henry... and it pops up when you open it!"

The woman began walking faster. Andrew stopped.

"Didn't you get any valentines?" he called after her. "Is that why you're cranky?

* * *

Remembering that their first meeting took place just before supper, Andrew decided the mysterious lady must take two walks every day. Clanging sounds from the kitchen was the signal he had prepared for. He wriggled into waiting boots and parka and slipped outside. When the last crow had been sent screaming to safety, the boy began his quest. He was three blocks away when he spotted her

"Hi! It's me." Andrew skidded to a stop beside her.

No response.

"What's your name, lady? I told you mine... Andrew."

The woman turned to a house they were passing and said nothing.

"Why won't you tell me your name? Please?"

"Lily," she said in a begrudging whisper.

"That's a flower's name," said the boy, wondering if perhaps that was what made her grow up odd. A moment later, he added, "Your mother must have used to like flowers, didn't she?"

The woman's hand moved hesitatingly toward Andrew's head, then immediately snapped back into its sleeve-cave.

"Did you ever marry a husband?" Andrew asked.

An almost imperceptible nod.

"Did you have any boys and girls then?"

Again the woman nodded.

"What kind?"

"Boys." Andrew could barely hear her voice.

"And did they... ?"

"They're away... gone!"

The unexpected volume and hardness in her voice frightened Andrew. He stopped walking. He covered his ears as she continued.

"You go away, too! Go home now. I walked *here* so you wouldn't follow me. Stay away from me. I can't like you."

* * *

That evening, while his father studied the newspaper and his mother washed dishes, Andrew grabbed his bat cape and crept back to the white square of lawn next to Lily's front steps. Biting his tongue for balance, and trying to maintain a clear view of the picture he carried in his mind, he stomped the outline of a huge heart in the snow. He was careful to aim the point toward the main window so that the drawing would make sense to its intended. He used full arm-swings to engrave "LOVE TO LILY" with his fat, mittened hand. In five giant steps he was back on the sidewalk, cape-gliding home.

By the time Andrew fell asleep that night, he was pretty much convinced that Lily was one of those "damsels" that Batman and Robin dedicated their lives to saving.

* * *

On Sunday morning, the bumpy valentine was still there. An anarchy of bird tracks had further decorated the heart, but his message was as he had left it. Andrew climbed the front steps and took a deep breath. Before he had time to knock, an explosion, of sorts, sent him sprawling. Snow and ice chunks struck his face, and a whirring black mass strafed his hair. The boy's fingers spread enough to look overhead. He ducked when a second crow thrashed aloft from the cornice above the door.

"Lily!" Andrew called, still on his knees.

No sound from within. He got to his feet and twisted the heavily carved doorknob. The door trembled loosely and opened a few inches.

"Lily?" he called again. His voice felt shrunken and sounded like it belonged to somebody else.

A Heart for Gypsy Lily

The old woman stood beside a chair in the large, otherwise empty room. "You may as well come in," she said, pushing the chair forward and making a gesture that Andrew decided was an invitation to sit. He knelt on the wooden seat and looked around the room with open mouth.

"Did you see my…" the boy began, once he had found his voice.

"I saw it," Lily snapped. "Thank you," she added in a softer voice.

After a long survey of the hollow room, Andrew spoke again. "Are you a damsel… or a gypsy?" he asked.

"A what?"

"A gyspy. They don't like furniture either. I saw some on television."

"Well," she replied, making a sound Andrew felt must be a laugh, "maybe that's what I am." She walked toward a door at the far end of the room. "You might be right," she said, stepping out of sight.

"Then I name you 'Gypsy Lily,' " Andrew called out.

She reappeared carrying a large glass of water. She handed it to the boy. "I've been called worse."

During none of his previous visits with grown-ups had he ever been served a glass of water. He sipped carefully, half expecting it to burn or to taste the way tambourines sound. Discovering it was just plain water, he took a big gulp, then asked his next question.

"But, where *did* your furniture go?"

Her reply was long in coming. When she finally spoke, her voice was dry and flat. "I had to eat. I sold it."

Andrew jumped up from the chair. "Gypsy Lily, are you a victim of crime? Because if you are, I will save you."

"Of crime?" she repeated, turning to stare out the window that overlooked Andrew's valentine. "Not everybody would call it 'crime.' " Turning back to the little boy, she added, "… but *I* would."

"I was right," Andrew shouted, "but now you are saved! I will wear my cape all the time from now on, and nobody can dare hurt you. We can be friends." He handed Lily the empty glass and strutted in a circle before her. "We'll be friends and play together every day after school. We'll go for walks and tell each other stuff. We can..."

The glass shattered on the bare floor. "Stop it!" Lily cried. Seeing Andrew's frightened expression, she lowered her voice. "Little Andrew, we cannot be friends." She held up a hand, commanding silence. "Be quiet and listen to me."

The outstretched hand and peculiar look on her face made Andrew obey.

"I am an old woman," she said, lowering her arm, "... much too old to play. You will find friends your own age soon. There are lots of children around. You'll find them, or they will find you, soon enough."

"But we could be friends *right now!*" Andrew insisted. "Let's just do it!"

"That's enough!" Lily said with finality. "I had little-boy friends at one time, and they went away. I've had big friends, too." She pressed a fragment of glass with her shoe. "They were, none of them, worth it." She bent forward, so that her eyes were on a level with Andrew's. "I don't want us to be friends. Believe that! Now go home."

* * *

Andrew stared at the caped crusaders dangling in the window. He reached out and snapped the string by which they were suspended. He put them under his bed. Sitting on the floor, using the full length of his leg, he pushed them out of sight.

In his dream, he and Henry were playing tag. Henry ducked behind a huge tree and Andrew couldn't find him, no matter how long or hard he tried.

* * *

A second boy jumped off the school bus when it pulled up to Andrew's house. They sat at each edge of the front stoop, kicking chunks of snow from the corners of the steps.

"You got a television in your room?" the boy asked.

A Heart for Gypsy Lily

"Nuh-uh," Andrew replied. "Let's make snow angels!"

"Are you kidding?" the boy scoffed. "That's baby stuff. Go get your guns. We'll play Army."

Andrew shook his head. He struggled to find an unembarrassing explanation for being weaponless, determined not to admit that his parents refused to allow him to have toy guns. Before he could think of what to say, the new boy stood up and said he had to go home. Andrew offered to walk along. Halfway into the second block, not saying a word to his companion, the boy began running. Fighting back tears, Andrew stood a few moments watching the retreating figure. Then he turned for home.

Rather than starting down his own block, Andrew walked to the far corner. Lily was sitting on her front steps. Hunched down in her black coat, she reminded Andrew of the Japanese snail that had lived for a week in his aquarium, and whose shell now rested in his box of marbles. There was something about the way she sat there that told the boy he would not be welcome.

Back in his room, Andrew knelt beside his bed and probed into the darkness beneath it. When his fingers failed to reached the desired objects, he gave up the search and, in a first-ever decision of its kind, Andrew climbed onto his bed to take a nap before supper.

* * *

"Are you going to spend this whole beautiful afternoon sitting indoors?" his mother asked on Saturday.

Andrew slid from his chair and was about to climb the stairs to his room when his mother, parting the curtains, said, "Who on earth is that?" He ran to the window, let out a yelp and ran for his jacket in the hallway.

Lily stood on the sidewalk with both hands pressed inside her sleeves. Andrew remained at the front door, unsure of what the odd look on the woman's face meant. Was she going to talk mean to him again? He took a deep breath, then skipped up to Lily and began exploring the furry cave of her sleeve. He withdrew one of her hands and wedged each of his fingers between hers. They started walking.

"Are we doing it?" Andrew asked. "Are we being friends now?"

"We're giving it a try," Lily answered.

A few steps later, squeezing the small digits that barely filled the spaces between her own, Lily spoke again.

"So, let's have it, little boy... tell me stuff."

The crows, perched along the gables on Lily's house, looking like a ragged lace border on an old-time greeting card, followed the travelers' progress with their tiny black eyes. Their heads moving in unison, the birds looked down at the sidewalk. Perhaps they were puzzled by the new patterns in the snow. Formerly, these side-by-side trails were identical, except for the sizes of the tracks. This time, one row showed the familiar straight-line dashes, but the second set looked different. The prints sometimes pointed inward, sometimes outward. At intervals, there were gaps— no tracks at all—as though the smaller trailblazer thought he too was a crow and was trying his hand at flying.

Caroline's Snake

1950

The words FREAK OF NATURE were scrawled at the top of each page in Caroline's girlhood diary. Teachers and parents tried comforting the unusually tall child with predictions of someday "growing into her bones," but she continued to suffer. When students at Beulah Elementary lined up before and after recess, Caroline bent her knees so that her shadow was cast over fewer standard-size children. At home and at school, the only two stages on which her life was played, she towered on the sidelines, desperate to escape her sideshow stardom and to simply blend into the crowd. It was the sense of being a displaced person that convinced Caroline, on her nineteenth birthday, to accept an uncle's job offer near the western tip of Lake Superior.

Westlund's Logging Camp had been transformed into a vacation lodge, and men flocked there for one-week slices of what they called "frontier life." Uncle Erik placed his niece in charge of the grub hall. On the first day, Caroline was dismayed to discover that she was the only female at the camp. By week's end, however, the last of her misgivings had evaporated. She found unexpected delight in watching the make-believe lumberjacks happily devouring mountains of potatoes while she turned sides of beef and venison into fuel for their pretended labors. She reveled in their bursts of applause and shouts of approval for her efforts.

By the time she reached middle age, the busy cook and hostess was satisfied with having found a safe and comfortable niche — a niche far surpassing her bleak girlhood expectations. She enjoyed organizing camp activities and dispensing the lightweight flirtations expected of her, but she maintained strict limits. Vacationers learned to respect the unspoken admonition: *Do Not Trespass.*

An exception appeared one morning in the form of a lanky fellow named Cyrus Lundine. The snowy-haired newcomer's manner was new to Caroline — oddly upsetting. No sly winking, none of the usual stylized bravura, only a calm and smiling self-assurance. She felt the power of Cy's personality, and she sensed danger.

Local musicians played old-time music on weekends, and one of Caroline's triumphs was convincing reticent campers to dance together. Describing the midwinter tedium of the old logging days, she told them that even the toughest lumberjacks "jigged each others' legs off" most nights after work was done. Her telling the tale always resulted in a flurry of shouting, stomping men, with Caroline as the sometimes-prize for a lucky dancer. Whenever Cy headed her way, she quickly grasped another's hand.

One morning, after setting down an enormous tray of flapjacks, she turned to find Cy standing beside her. Before she could formulate some kind of neutral greeting, the grinning man raised his hand and said, "We'll talk tonight." So saying, he strode out of the grub hall.

That evening, after prolonging chores as much as possible, the nervous hostess sat across a table from the man who so jostled her mind. He poured beers from an ironstone pitcher and slid one toward Caroline. He looked at her for an alarming few minutes before speaking.

"How long, do you think, before you give in... and like me?"

Caroline took a long swig of beer.

"I asked your uncle if he knew how come you're chilly to me. He said he couldn't imagine, unless maybe you had a thing against big, pointy Adam's apples."

Caroline laughed, despite her determination not to.

"I didn't think that was it," Cy said, shaking his head with mock relief. "You don't strike me as an apple bigot."

Laughter eventually did away with Caroline's tensed shoulder muscles, and by evening's end they had spent two hours in easy conversation. It wasn't until Cy brought up deeper matters — private thoughts and feelings — that her old barriers began reas-

Caroline's Snake

sembling themselves. Thanking him for the evening, Caroline hurried to the stairway. Before taking the first step, Cy, who was then beside her, spoke several stunning sentences.

"We're a match, you know," he said matter-of-factly. "Couldn't be plainer."

Caroline opened her mouth to protest, but Cy raised his hand.

"Don't," he said. "The idea needs hatching time, I know. We'll have another go at it this fall."

When Caroline came downstairs the next morning, Cy had already left the lodge.

During the month between the camp's summer and autumn seasons, Caroline was freed from her regular duties. Unlike other years, this hiatus proved anything but restful for her. Cy's face and final words plagued her brain. How did he dare say that to her? "A match?" What was that supposed to mean? He certainly didn't expect her to... Why, she would no more dream of... Foolishness. What nonsense!

Alone in the evenings, she often stood at her mirror.

"Maybe you're not happy with your life. Is that it?"

"Of course I'm happy! I fit here. I belong."

"But isn't this just a different version of the old days—still starring in a kind of freak show?"

Whenever the demands of her reflection became too frightening, Caroline resorted to the familiar "Uncle Erik needs me."

The first wave of blue-jeaned, butt-slappin', cud-chewin' urbanites arrived the first week of September, and the old lightheartedness returned to Caroline. She fed on the jokes and fast-spinning banter, flirted innocently and accepted the traditional gallantries.

Midweek, days before she might have expected such a thing, Cy stepped into the kitchen. He removed his jacket without a word, grabbed a paring knife and joined Caroline at the tower of potatoes on the workbench.

"How've you been, Caroline?"

"I've been fine."

"Have you been thinking about me?" Cy ventured.

"Yes." She spoke as though admitting a defeat.

"Been thinking about *you?*" Cy continued.

"About me?"

He stopped peeling a potato and looked directly at Caroline. "Well, there ain't much more to me than what you see." He began working on the potato again. "You're the one with a mystery to solve."

"What mystery, Cyrus?"

"You got a closed-tight space inside you, dearie. There's a snake got a burrow right near where your heart beats. I was wondering if maybe you caught a glimpse of him while I was away. Funny thing about them heart-snakes," he added with a quiet chuckle, "once they get pushed into the light, they generally skedaddle."

"Can't you say it plain, Cy?"

"Don't you know the name of that thing padlocked inside you, Caroline? You got to name it. That's the way to unhook the cage and shuck the nasty varmint out."

They loaded the kettles of boiling water without further words. As she dried the workbench, Cy cleared his throat several times.

"I'd like to be your partner at the dance tomorrow night. Think you could bear such a thing?"

"I believe I could bear it," she answered.

Caroline moved to the stove, lifted a gigantic wooden ladle, whirlpooled the tumbling potatoes, and pictured vipers in her bosom.

The dance was a noisy glory. The band performed with a thumping energy that seemed to increase as the evening wore on. The floor filled with men who swirled and leapt, stamped and bellowed, kicked heels and slapped thighs. Cy and Caroline kept up with them, only occasionally flopping onto chairs to recover their breaths. When, around midnight, athletic prowess began to crumble, the band—perhaps noticing the exclusive partnership of Cy and their hostess—switched to a gentle waltz. The sweating men, unwilling to go so far as to dance *slow* with each other, shuffled toward the tables and the welcome beer.

Alone on the dance floor, the couple swayed in long ovals without speaking. Caroline broke the silence.

"I got hold of that snake last night."

"You did? He bite you?"

"No. He tried, though."

When Caroline had returned to her room the previous night, she spent time at her mirror—her thinking post. She then removed photo albums from her bedside book shelves and arranged them on the bed. The pictorial tour stretched from babyhood to Uncle Erik's last birthday. After closing the cover of the last album, she took a deep breath and unlocked a small drawer in her dressing table.

The diary had a ruined clasp. The pages were yellowed and photographs had been wedged between them. Throughout her years at home, Caroline had pilfered the most unattractive pictures she could find of herself from her parents' collection and had organized them in documentary fashion—inarguable proofs of the grotesque oddity she knew herself to be. Caroline dislodged the photos and carefully tore each page from the binding. Slowly, one by one, the contents were folded and refolded into neat, compact rectangles.

"That snake was in a book I had."

"A book, huh?" Cy marveled, halting their dance for two beats before resuming. "I guess they can hide just about anyplace. Did you remember to feed it?"

"No."

"It still up there?"

"Nuh-uh. I murdered it… cooked its goose… tossed it in the fireplace."

"Miss it?"

"Not at all."

"Wanna marry me, then?"

"You bet I do."

Cy let out a yelp that stopped the band and brought the resting dancers to their feet. In a voice caroling with joy, he raised his sweetheart's hand and told the crowd they were beholding the any-minute-now Missus Cyrus Lundine. The musicians launched into "Carolina in the Morning," while the guests whooped and stamped their approval. With mugs in hand, and with arcs of brew crisscrossing the air, a raucous jubilee jig was danced in honor of the embracing couple.

Cy drove to Westlund's Camp for the last time in early November. Uncle Erik and a minister's sister were witnesses at the simple wedding ceremony in Oliver. Cy taped boxes in his new bride's room while she and her uncle took a long walk through the grounds where Caroline had grown from a girl into a woman. Two cardboard boxes and a wicker basket easily accommodated the retiring hostess's thirty-year accumulation of personal belongings.

When the newlyweds moved into their stucco house in South Beulah, Mrs. Lundine found she was busier than she had anticipated. They looked up many of Caroline's "long lost" relatives, made periodic raids on nearby antique and book shops, and bought a puppy they named, "Erik the Red." Caroline's major project that winter was learning to cook for two instead of fifty.

Sometimes, when Cy was out of the house, Caroline paused before the hallway mirror and tried to find that one-time Freak of Nature.

"What on earth is it," she would demand of the smiling reflection, "that makes a person's bones shrink when they're not paying attention?"

One day, an astonishing thing happened. In Cy-like tones, the image in the mirror answered her question.

"Well, first off I'll tell you what it isn't. The cure for Big Bone Problems isn't either hiding out or blending in. No, Ma'am," the reflection lectured. "It begins by shucking all heart-snakes in the vicinity."

It struck Caroline that the voice was much too Cy-like to be springing from her own head. She scanned the deep space of the mirror as the voice continued.

"Once you locate and name the culprit, it's not that hard to shuck it out. Then, all that's left to do is track down the best looking man on this ball of earth and talk him into marrying you. Next thing you know, every single one of your bones will…"

Caroline was at the hall door in seconds flat. No Cy! She ran through every room, commanding him to turn himself in, but he was not to be found. At suppertime, Cy played innocent. He never did, in fact, admit to impersonating a looking glass, and Caroline gave up asking for his confession.

Caroline's Snake

Though they never again discussed it outright, the incident was kept alive and in healthy condition by the anniversary cards they exchanged each year.

One envelope was addressed to: "Cyrus, Cyrus, on the Wall."

The other said: "To the Fairest in the Land."

South Beulah, Minnesota   Harold Huber

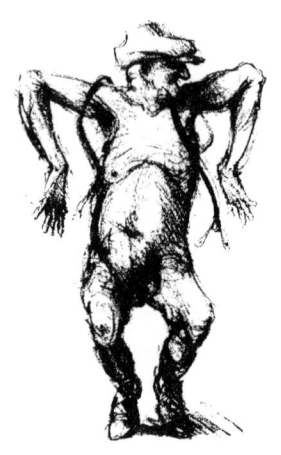

A Cowboy's Sweetheart

1936

In 1929 the stock market crashed and Mrs. Miller became pregnant. Bread lines formed and so did her baby. When 1930 limped in, two important christenings had taken place. The era was named "The Depression," and the Millers' boy (me) was named William... Billy.

In the usual manner of recently-borns, I ignored the nation's plight and the ripple effects in my own community of South Beulah, Minnesota. I left things like depressions to my elders while I concentrated on more vital matters. Eating, pronouncing words, memorizing endless numbers of them, seeking maximum attention, becoming familiar with my body parts and covering those parts with grime... these were my concerns. Sitting on the drainboard of our kitchen sink with my feet immersed in a dishpan of suds is my clearest recollection of that decade's first years.

By 1935 I caught on to the concept of relating the incidents of one moment to those of another, and thereby began recognizing a shape to my life. People, happenings, judgments and memories began clustering around me in heaps as high, but not nearly as fascinating, as those in the town dump beyond our alley.

The dump was my private Land of Wonders. Every moment of freedom from my parents or sitters was spent in those miraculous humps of man-made Nature, studying and enjoying. What *couldn't* be learned there? It was a University of Junk—of battered kettles, legless stoves, ruined boots, partial game boards, wounded mattresses, orphaned dolls and dazzling unnameable clues to the past. Archaeology had me by the scruff of the soul and wouldn't let go. The belief that all I surveyed there was at least a hundred layers deep, and that all was mine for the mere digging, made me itchy for each next return to paradise.

Our home had a name. It was "The OK Inn." My father said it was a tavern with an eat-counter. Mother spoke of it as "the restaurant." It stood, or rather, sat, at the south end of Euclid Avenue where the "real" town ended and the stockyards took over. During daylight hours, the inn held a smattering of recently freed prisoners of Prohibition. But at sundown, the numbers swelled and it became a living ragtime symphony conducted by my parents and their three part-time helpers.

Charlie Bucker tended bar out front, along with my father. He was unmarried—a condition that counted against him in South Beulah. At his age? Twenty-nine?!

Diane Gehrke assisted my mother in the kitchen and also served as baby sitter. Diane introduced me to hatred. I loathed this beast. I called her "The Scump." I wished to see her tortured and beheaded.

Snowball was the sole black employee at The OK Inn and the sole black resident of our town. He stumbled onto Euclid Avenue one night, from whence no one could imagine, drunk and lost. Naturally, he was thrown in jail. For the next three decades he cleaned the jailhouse in return for a permanent home in one of the cells. Early each morning he scrubbed the floors, lunch counter and bar at our place, then did the same at a few other establishments. He became Euclid's pet oddity and, because of his quiet wit and honorable ways, did much to ruin long-held prejudices. The police chief knew his given name but, for some reason, refused to divulge it. When asked directly about his real name, Snowball winked and pantomimed packing snow in his hand, then tossing it. He and Willyboo (his nickname for me) were such good friends that I had permission to call him "Snow."

On those blessed occasions when Diane was unavailable, Aunt Bruna was called upon to help in the kitchen or to Billy-sit—jubilee nights for me. I loved Aunt Bruna. She was the very opposite of The Scump. She always laughed, hadn't a single witch-tendency and usually toted a book of stories and a jar of Ovaltine in her huge red purse. In my world, she was the only serious rival to the dump.

A Cowboy's Sweetheart

We lived in quarters behind the kitchen, but I spent as much time as was allowed "out front" — as close to the bar as possible. I became the *little darling* of the daytime crowd and spent, at their parent-overriding insistence, many hours at the pin ball machine. From them I learned that money was made out of nickels. I also learned that the number of nickels pressed into my greedy fists depended on the number of times they asked my father or Charlie for a refill. I became rather a crack master at guiding steel balls into scoring holes... which meant *more nickels!*

The long mahogany bar was higher than my head, unless I stood tiptoed on the rail along its base. When thus perched with my chin hooked on the bar top, I drank in the wonderful sights... golden bottles of liquor, lumpy cellophane bags of pretzels, colossal jars of pickled eggs, a scolding cardboard finger warning, "No cash — no drink," and a star-framed picture of President Roosevelt. Whenever my father was too busy to notice, I climbed to this vantage point, in spite of two terrible dangers: one to life and limb, the other to my psyche.

Because bar-hooking required the ultimate stretch from neck to toe, I sometimes found myself back on the floor with a bruised lip or bitten tongue. The second danger was by far the worse. Spaced at even intervals under the foot rail were six brass spittoons. Many times, in hideous fascination, I watched a glistening clot shoot from a customer's mouth and disappear with a sickening splash into the black recess of a polished vessel. Every bar-hook was preceded by a check on spitting locations. Even then, appalling pictures streaked across my mind. One time, after an especially awkward slip, my foot caused one of the spittoons to rock and wobble. When it finally rattled to rest without tipping over, I ran to my room and told God I'd never be bad again.

Because it was beautiful and inspiring and safe from spit, my very most favorite spot out front was at our giant jukebox, which stood as big and solid as Sophie Tucker in the center of the open floor. On Friday and Saturday nights it was surrounded by dancing couples, but during my hours, it stood alone — waiting — glowing pink and blue from within. Brought to life by my nickel collection, it swept me into the clouds on the golden vibratos of Tex Ritter, Lullabelle and Scotty, the Sons of the Pioneers and —

most cloud-sweeping of all—Patsy Montana.

Sometimes I felt it was my nose, not the steel needle, that was sliding through the grooves, grinding those skinny ditches into gray powder. The spinning record label told me which tune was coming before the music even started. I knew the words to every song and all the nuances of each singer's voice. Indoor afternoons usually found me pressed into the jukebox's vibrating bosom or, if it were Patsy Montana's turn, weaving a solo waltz around its base.

I was happy with my adventures inside, but none of their allurements quite measured up to the siren call of the dump. It was there, alone with my imagination, life could be lived to its five-year-old fullest.

On July 18th, 1936, I turned six. It was the day I discovered that living life to its six-year-old fullest would have its baleful side. Because I wasn't unusually psychic, I started that morning as though it were to be like all the others. I slid from the sheets, did with my flattened palm what I called "making the bed," pulled on my ravaged short pants and headed for the kitchen. To my profound disgust, The Scump was already there.

She had revealed her true colors the very first day she was hired to keep an eye on me. For some completely unjustifiable reason, she twisted my ear and called me a sneaky scamp. I informed her that she was a sneaky scump, and since the explosive syllable seemed to fit her to a "T," I addressed her by that name—with gratifying results—forever after. Having decided not to waste one birthday minute on her, but still needing a proper parting gesture, I ejected a silvery puddle of spit at her feet... wishing to my toenails it could be a spittoon-splasher... and ran off to my beloved dump.

Just as I became involved in my day's work, a gunshot cracked the air. I ducked behind the husk of a Model T and waited for Death. When I worked up the nerve to uncrouch, I saw two rough looking boys lurching among the trash heaps, each with a BB gun. At intervals they hunched over their weapons and fired a shot at one of the many resident rats. I was shocked at their depravity, since I had planned to one day capture one of those very rats, tame and train it, and name it Renfro. Finally, in gradually dimi-

A Cowboy's Sweetheart

nishing cascades of whoops and war cries, they disappeared into a further valley, and I resumed construction of my house. Architecture had become my "calling" for the day.

Two propped-up, rusted car hoods formed my roof. Beneath it, assembled for my living ease, were two shadeless lamps, most of an armchair, a one-doored toaster, a Shirley Temple glass, much of a deck of cards, a Camel Pack with one remaining cigarette (this was big!) and a punch-board with three "punches" still wedged in place. I began searching for the two missing items, a match for the Camel and a long, skinny anything for the punches. I found instead... a dime. A devil coin.

All thoughts of architecture vanished as I ran home to show off my treasure. Used to nickels as I was, that dime represented incomprehensible wealth to me. I climbed the mounds of rubble as fast as scab-hampered knees allowed, and when I reached the alley I switched to a gallop, hi-hoed Silver, and paced myself to Rossini. The back door slammed with a mighty crack as I rushed into the kitchen holding the glinting coin at arm's length. Before I could shift from exultation to standard defensive tactics, The Scump snatched the dime from my fingers.

"Where'd you get this?"

"I found it in the dump. It's old buried treasure."

"It is not. It's brand new. It says, '1936'."

I didn't know you could *read* money, but I didn't let on.

"You tell me this minute... where'd you get it?"

"I told you! Give it back or I'll get the men with guns to come and shoot you."

"Men with guns? Billy Miller, don't you lie to me!"

"It's not a lie. There's two of them... with guns. They're shooting and killing in the dump. Gimme my dime or I'll tell them to plug you like a rat!"

"Billy!"

"It's the truth. They killed one already!"

The good old dependable Scump let out a curdler, and a moment later my mother and father and Charlie and all the daytime regulars were crowded around me, looking frightened... waiting for me to speak. It was then that the goddess, Drama, o'ertook me. She sank her fangs deeply and injected her sweet nectar.

~ 29 ~

Inspired by this occurrence, and out of the twin needs to save face and disallow a triumph for The Scump, I created a grand fiction—a monument of fiction—as opposed to the piddling fibs of day-to-day survival.

Each pressing question from my stunned audience caused new details to be added. YES, a man had been shot... *three* times! NO. The body wasn't still out there... people in a *green* car had hauled it away. Did I see it all? YES. Had *they* seen me? NO. Was I telling the truth? YEESSS!!

When the whirlwind of invention had spun itself out, I found I was in the police chief's office at the jailhouse. Father sat beside me as I whispered answers to the huge man's questions. I told and retold the "facts," gradually subtracting a few of what seemed like the more dangerous ones. I was given many opportunities to take back the entire story, but with my father's eyes upon me, I held firm. At one point, the chief gestured for my father to leave the room, and as he did so, Snowball walked past and looked in. His eyes said, "I pity you, Willyboo," and I hid my face in my hands.

The chief closed the door, then rolled his desk chair next to mine. He sat facing me, his gigantic hand covering my knee. That warmth on my shivering skin and the kindly expression on the old man's face reversed the current. Truth shot out of me like the spills at Niagra... that is, if truthful head-nods can be compared with waterfalls.

I hadn't really seen a murder, had I? (up and down)

I only wanted to scare the sitter into giving my dime back... wasn't that it? (up and down)

But it was fun making up the story... one *that good*, right? (up and down, vigorously)

And I truly hadn't wanted to make my mother and father worry so bad... wasn't that right?

I saw a tear hit the chief's hand as I shook my head as hard as I could. I answered his last question in words.

"No, I don't know what perjury is, but I'm sure I don't want to do it, or be it, or make any. I only want to go home now. I promise to never tell lies again, so can't I please go home and not to jail?"

A Cowboy's Sweetheart

At the station door, Father shook the chief's hand, then, without a word to me, we began the four-block walk to The OK Inn. I tried doubly hard to avoid cracks on the sidewalk, figuring it would be bad enough facing my mother without breaking her back in the bargain. My father pushed the big front door open and I, fighting back tears, ducked under his arm and crept inside. I tried not to look up, but my eyes did it anyway.

Mother stood behind the lunch counter talking with Aunt Bruna. They looked at me, then out of merciful kindness, they began arranging glasses and cups on the shelves. The regulars turned from their beers to stare. One man spat. They followed my father to the back end of the bar to hear his whispered report. Snowball opened the door of the ladies room, wiped his eyes and disappeared inside with his mop and bucket. Diane was leaning against the pin ball machine with her arms crossed. Before my eyes dropped back to the floor, they snagged on The Scump's just long enough to receive her victory smile.

With a severely burdened heart, I walked slowly to Sophie Tucker and pressed my body to her warm, bulging curve. That did it. The dry spell broke. Skinny trails of teardrops looked pink on the glowing glass.

The impact of my embrace (or God) then did something quite remarkable. The works within the jukebox began to rumble and creak. Before my chastened eyes, an old shellac record was girdled by a metal hoop, snatched from its row, lifted vertically, turned horizontally, then dropped with a thud on the revolving turntable. After the grinding prelude of the outer rim, Patsy Montana, in the comfort of her clover-honey tones, confided to me that all she required for restored happiness was to be a cowboy's sweetheart.

Me too! Me too!
I needed to be somebody's sweetheart, too.
Some old cowboy's.
Anybody's!

South Beulah, Minnesota   Harold Huber

The Twins

1951

Between sips of coffee, Myrtle shook her head and grumbled. "Myrle and Myrtle—such names! How could Ma and Pa have done that to us?"

Myrle stiffened, stabbed a frown between her sister's eyes, but said nothing. Having received no counter-punch, Myrtle shrugged one shoulder and lifted her cup with a satisfied grin.

The women had never lived apart. They were bound together by seventy years of shared environments, mutual rites and reciprocal features. Farm poverty early in the century had made the roots of competition woody, tough and deep. Which identical dress, sewn from the season's flour sacks, would have a slight winning edge of some sort? Which girl would help cook for the thrashers on Lundgren's farm, which stay home with Ma to bake, wash clothes and wield the flat-iron? These were equally despicable options, until one voiced a preference. Then the battle was on.

"Well, I have got to admit you don't look seventy, Em."

Myrle waved her off impatiently, but was secretly pleased. "Neither do you, Myrt, but you do act it lately." Immediately regretting the hostile tone she'd allowed in her voice, she quickly added, "But I guess we got a right to act it... or any other way, for that matter."

That did it. The gong didn't sound. Round One did not commence.

"You know, we'll really be seventy-one at eight o'clock."

Myrtle instantly sobered and demanded, "Where do you get that foolishness from?" She clenched her teeth as a familiar condescending inflection glided into her sister's voice.

"Well, when your birthday comes, you're really a year older than it says."

"Myrle, that's crazy talk."

"It most certainly ain't crazy talk at all. On your first birthday, you've already been alive a whole year, and you're into your second one."

"Myrle Anderson!"

"Everybody knows that, Myrtle."

"Well, I never met a grown-up person who ever thought such a thing."

"Well, how many grown-ups you figure *you* meet in a month?"

"Well, may I ask you what that's just supposed to mean?"

"Well, you can ask until you're purple in the gills, Miss!"

Round One was launched.

No matter what the intensity or duration of these matches, they were not allowed to interfere with the twins' several traditional rituals. Therefore, evening found them pressing the doorbell of their cousin, Cy Lundine's, home, where their annual natal celebrations took place. The generous bulk of Caroline, Cy's wife, filled the door frame.

"My lands! Lookit you! If it ain't the birthday girls!"

Both women were then engulfed in yards of dotted swiss. They had tried for years to resist this "outsider" who, twenty summers before, returned with their cousin from one of his lumberjack vacations as Mrs. Cyrus Lundine. Strong-willed as the twins were, they proved no match for the openhearted good nature of their new relative. They had to give in, and now spoke of her as, "meaning well."

"Cy!" the jolly woman shouted over her shoulder, "The birthday gals are here!"

A high, gritty voice curved from a doorway down the hall where a TV-blue light cast a rectangle on the wall.

"Just git on in here," the voice commanded, "… and git your spankins!"

Six female eyes met in anticipatory delight. The threesome aimed their shoes toward the only man in their lives—the only adult male they knew who wasn't a total fool.

The Twins

Cy was ten years older than the twins. He was a six-foot stack of shoulder blades, knees, knuckles and white hair. He had been the twins' chief playmate in childhood and was the Anderson's mainstay when Pa died of influenza. He made sure the girls stayed in high school when Ma joined her husband, and he got them their very first housekeeping jobs. As the clacking of high heels in the hallway grew louder, Cy struggled out of his chair, leaving a frieze cast-mold of his boney back and bottom. When the women entered, his eyes struck light, and two bear paws shot forward.

In the next moment, 1910 slipped into the room as a merry, shrieking free-for-all ensued. Myrle and Myrtle pushed furniture and dodged into temporary safety zones, while Cy attempted to deliver his birthday wallops. Ten minutes later, everyone was seated in the dining room, staring at the gargantuan banquet Caroline had created in honor of her matched in-laws. As the meal progressed , major news items and neighborhood reports were hotly debated by the celebrating combatants, while Caroline acted as referee.

At a pre-planned moment, Caroline slipped into the kitchen and Cy began singing an old Swedish birthday carol. The twins called a truce, nervously cleared their throats and prepared themselves to be surprised. When Caroline reappeared, she held before her a huge cake decorated in Rococo style. Seven tiny candle flames were pulled dotted-swissward as she joined her alto to Cy's shaky tenor and completed the procession to the table. "One for each decade!" she trilled as with well-practiced accuracy she placed the festal offering at an exact midpoint between the birthday girls. Myrtle and Myrle "oohed" and "for heaven saked" into the gleeful gazes of their cousins. Their own eyes remained mutually unencountered.

When Caroline and Myrtle moved to the kitchen with stacks of bowls and plates, Cy gestured for Myrle to remain.

"What's goin' on with you and Myrt?"

"I have no idea what you mean, Cyrus."

Myrle fussed with her scatter pins. She bit her lower lip, folded and refolded the corners of her place mat. When she looked up, a crescent of liquid glinted along each lid.

"There's a thing called 'saturation,' Cy. That's what's the matter. We did wrong, Cy, living together all these years."

The old man, suddenly aware that he was hearing words long kept padlocked in dark, private places, withheld his "acting the goose" comment and remained silent.

"You've got no idea what it's like, being a double. Looking at a copy of yourself. Only it's not you. It's a fake you, saying stupid and foolish... Twins ain't right, Cy. They are God's big mistake."

"You mean to tell me you don't like your very own sister? Seventy years later you decide you don't like her, just like that?"

"Oh, Cy. It ain't 'just like that.' It ain't at all. Myrtle has hated me all our lives. She makes that quite clear every single day."

Cy shook his head as Myrle listed the ways her sister proved her enmity.

In the kitchen, dishwashing progressed in a lurch-pause-lurch manner.

"Well, have you two talked these things out?"

"You mean *like grown-ups?* Caroline, we're speaking about Myrle. You can't talk sense to her!"

"Honey, you can. Have you tried... really tried? You ain't become so different from each other as all that."

"See... you think just like everyone else. We only look alike, Cary. Nothing else... not anymore. And besides, what's the use of all that trying with someone you know hates you?"

"I don't know what to say."

"There's nothing you need say. I'm going to move out. I'll get my own place and start living my own life. I ain't too old to do that, and I *am* old enough to know you go away from where you ain't appreciated."

Once the foursome had settled in the sitting room, and in spite of the badly damaged festive mood, Cy successfully launched their customary get-together rite. The magic words were, "Girls, do you remember... ?" The question, as always, proved irresistible, and soon the predictable, comfortable tales from the farm returned to life. Myrle's and Myrtle's accounts were so lacerated and entangled from challenges and corrections of detail, that all breathed easier when Cy had the platform.

In the middle of the story of Ma's twenty-loaves-of-bread marathon, Cy stopped short. His face seemed to flatten and turn

The Twins

gray. He lurched forward and fell on his knees. The three women were instantly around him. "Oh God!" Caroline cried as she took his face in her hands. Myrle smoothed his damp hair and Myrtle patted his hand.

"Cy honey, where does it hurt?"

"Just be calm, dear."

"Should we get the doctor?"

"Is it any better now, love?"

Cy lowered himself onto the braided rug and slowly rolled to his back. When normal color began returning and his drawn lips relaxed into a weak grin, they helped him into the beloved blue chair.

"Oh Cy, what *was* that?" asked Myrle in a shaken voice.

"You mustn't keep one thing from us, Cyrus," Myrtle sobbed. She brushed a stray lock from his forehead. "Remember, you're our only family. You are all we got left, now."

The old man patted his wife's knee as she half-sat on the broad arm of his chair. He reached forward and took one hand of each twin.

"Family?" Cy asked, squeezing the fingers he held. "Why, you surely know that family is a on-loan thing, not a for-keeps thing. Cary and me, we feel awful grateful that we still got four little chunks of family left. Not everybody our age is so lucky. But that ain't what I wanted to tell you. It's this thing I know, that you don't." He released the twins' hands, sat up straight and folded his arms. " So pay attention."

For the second time that evening, the early part of the century swept in to envelop Myrlc and Myrtle. Once again, two gawky farm girls stood before their surrogate father — obedient, chastened, ready to be scolded and instructed.

"You two got to make up your minds about this twin stuff. Get it clear so's you can quit drivin' each other — and all the rest of us — crazy. You say that people act as if you wasn't each your own person, but it seems to me *you both* are the worst committers of that sin. 'Think like me... exactly like me... in every single way... or else!' That's the message I hear ricochetin' back and forth between you."

The twins swapped sidelong glances. Caroline shifted so that

~ 37 ~

Cy's head rested against her shoulder.

"Now, here's what I wanted you to know. When mealtime used to come around," Cy's voice had thinned to a pensive softness, "your mama used to give you her pretty round titty, each at a different time, no matter how loud the other hollered. She understood that her little squirmy look-alikes were not two halves of a single baby, but two separate trouble-makers, each runnin' on its own kind of battery. But here's the most interestin' part of that story. Aunt Belle used to have to sit in your Pa's big rocker and hold the two of you together—one heavy lump of you in each arm with your fat pink feet all wound and jumbled together—before you'd stop fussin' and go to sleep. I'd be awful surprised if there ain't a lesson in there, someplace..." Cy stretched forward to tap the end of Myrle's then Myrtle's nose with the tip of his once-calloused forefinger, "... awful surprised."

In the first minutes of their walk home that evening, neither twin spoke.

Myrtle was the first to break the silence.

"We *are* the worst committers—like Cy says—ain't we, Em?"

"We are."

"And lucky—like he says, too—still having some real family."

"Luckier than we deserve! Seventy solid years of concern and caring from that darling man."

"And we mustn't forget Caroline," Myrtle said with conviction.

"You're so right, Myrt," Myrle concurred. "If anyone in this world ever *meant well*, it's that dear girl."

"Absolutely."

They shifted purses to their outer arms so that they could hold hands as they continued their journey home.

"Wasn't that sweet, the way Cy scolded us."

"Sweet as maple candy, Em. And wasn't that precious, the way he patted our cheeks when he said, 'awful surprised'?"

"More precious than gold, dear. But you mean tickled our chins, not patted our cheeks."

"Well, it doesn't much matter, does it?" Myrle asked, bearing down slightly on the fingers trapped between her own.

"The Twins"

"Of course it doesn't, dear," Myrtle answered calmly, "except, the fact is…"

"The fact? And have we been elected Fact Keeper, now?"

"And just exactly what is that supposed to mean?"

"You have all the *facts*… you tell me!"

"Well, Miss. You can just wonder about that until you're purple in the gills!"

"Oh yes? Well you can just…"

"Oh yes? Well, you might…"

"Oh yes? Well then…"

"Oh yes? Well…"

"Oh yes?…"

"Oh…"

South Beulah, Minnesota   Harold Huber

Chapter Three

1960

Ordinarily, during the daytime, Norval could see through the picture, as one sees beyond reflected images in a window display. But there were times when the picture ceased to be transparent and became frighteningly clear. It might happen any time — at dinner with his foster parents, inside the washers and dryers he cleaned at the laundromat, unfailingly in the night. It was then, in the black space above his pillow, or buried deep within it, the scene became solid and life-size. It was then he stood *in* the picture.

Red earth, red lights, red everything. A bloodied hammer in the grass. His sister, Alva, lying prone, scarlet streaks in her hair and on her lifeless outstretched arm. In the background, his father in handcuffs, staring from the sheriff's rear car window — the too-open, drunken eyes that had terrified Norval every day of his life.

Norval came to believe others somehow saw the terrible vision when they looked in his eyes. Surely that explained their averted gazes, the tongue-tied clutch and worsening stammer he experienced during encounters, even with longtime friends. But now he had a plan to change all that.

It was Norval's eighteenth birthday, the day of his escape from South Beulah. He had saved enough from his job at the laundromat to buy his first-ever car. The gas tank was full, and a long letter of thanks and farewell lay in plain sight on his foster parents' kitchen table. He would drive and drive until he found some unhaunted place where dream-ghosts were not allowed to stalk and terrify.

Having no specific destination in mind, Norval turned onto the first highway with which he was unfamiliar. At the outskirts

South Beulah, Minnesota Harold Huber

of a town called Ellison, his eyes were slapped by a gaudy, hand-painted sign proclaiming, "ELLISON ART FAIR—LEFT ON HWY. 7." Realizing there was no reason not to, he headed down the gravel trunk road and soon caught sight of colored banners shimmying in the sunlight.

Two middle-aged women stood hand-in-hand outside a main tent, next to an old man playing an accordion. Their slender soprano voices wove in and out of "Beautiful Isle of Somewhere." When the song ended, they rushed to Norval, bade him welcome and, pointing to a narrow tent nearby, instructed him to look-look-look and buy-buy-buy. He politely headed in the direction of their parallel forefingers.

The art works were arranged on sawhorse tables. Their prices ranged from twenty to fifty dollars. He was surprised, therefore, to find a group of paintings, all by the same artist, marked at one dollar. They were peculiar pictures, long and very narrow—stripes of images. Nature objects and rows of hand-holding figures patterned the horizontal rectangles. Floating over these forms—larger than anything else depicted—was a solitary animal casting shadows in many directions. "Dream-like," Norval said to himself. A voice from some deeper part of his brain added, "Like *other* people's dreams."

Norval was puzzled by the powerful effect the paintings had on him. One in particular tugged at something inside, and he decided to own it. "I'm buying my first art!" he marveled, fingering the meager contents of his new wallet. He handed a dollar bill to the women in charge and asked about the artist. Well yes... they supposed Olvine *was* interesting... in her odd way. She lived two miles down the road. Oh no... no possibility of missing the place... three ramshackle buildings that never knew a lick of paint. As Norval climbed into the car, the women waved halfheartedly, shaking their heads in unison.

When the flapping banners were out of sight, Norval pulled off the road. He lifted the painting from the seat beside him, stepped out and placed it on the car hood. How could something so strange feel so right? Why the huge suspended turtle? Did its radiating shadows have meaning? Why, with each answerless question, was he loving this narrow panel more and more?

Chapter Three

Thoroughly amazed by the bolt of decision shooting through him, Norval propped the picture above the back seat so that it was framed in the rear-view mirror and drove down a gravel lane to meet the artist, Olvine.

Three buildings, nestled in a dip in the land, came into view. They glowed with the silver-gray sheen of weathered wood. When Norval turned off the ignition, he felt it again... the thin steel cable tightening somewhere deep in his throat. He sat for a moment with closed eyes, both hands clutching the wheel. "Not this time!" he said aloud, then stepped from the car.

A row of pickets fronted the property. Norval lifted the wire hoop on the fence post, pushed against the squawking gate and walked toward the house. While mounting the porch step, he noticed a ring of small crosses in the grass. He recognized them from the painting he carried. For an instant, Alva's white gravestone appeared in the center of the ring.

The few times Norval had come upon a sight of unexpected beauty, he experienced a kind of aching in his chest. It happened when he saw Olvine's picture at the fair, and he felt it again looking into the face behind the screen door. Its delicate features were engraved by tiny wrinkles. The woman's white hair was brushed from her face and folded into a loose bun. Her hands were framed against a flowered apron.

"You selling something," she asked, "or are you a real person?"

Norval's hand shook as he lifted the picture. So did his voice. "Your painting... I bought it... I wanted to..."

"You're real," she interrupted, clicking her tongue. "Come on in. We'll talk. There's fresh coffee."

The pleasing ache intensified as Norval followed the old woman into the center of what seemed a huge painting. The walls were covered, from furniture tops to the ceiling, with long, narrow pictures. Where no furniture stood, the panels reached to the baseboards. After pouring coffee, Olvine watched the boy's astonished survey of the room.

"You see from the soul," she said calmly. "That's good. You'll have a proper life."

She sat at the kitchen table and pointed to the two steaming cups. Norval hesitated a moment, then joined her. The old woman's expression said to him, "Relax. You're safe."

"You don't know what to say about the paintings. That's natural... how could you? I don't trust those who know what to say about art. It's all in the eyes and what they're connected to... not in the vocal cords."

They finished their coffee with no further conversation. Olvine hummed quietly and studied her guest, as he squinted to see paintings on a far wall. She stood and, with a sweeping arm gesture, indicated he should continue his tour.

One after the other, Norval looked into the private visions of the only artist he'd ever met. He was unable to interpret his feelings... no words came to mind. It wasn't his old tongue-tying devil this time. That sensation was gone... perhaps because he knew she really didn't expect him to speak.

"What's your name?" Olvine called from the stove.

"Norval Ferguson."

"Mine's Olvine Ansgaard. Good one, isn't it?" she chuckled, sliding the coffeepot back to the hot lid on the range. She called to him again.

"Are you religious, Norval?"

After a minute's struggle with the question, Norval said, "I guess not... not very."

"Me neither," she responded, "But I do love God. That's one reason I paint," she added. "Seems only right... 'thanks for life,' you know."

Norval had never before felt so at ease with someone, other than his sister, Alva. His mind was filling with questions he would not be afraid to ask. This unusual woman had somehow, in only a few minutes, made a straight connection with him. He silently blessed the Ellison Art Fair.

Laughing as she did so, Olvine refilled their cups and waved Norval back to the table.

"*Now* let's talk," she said.

"I like... I love your paintings, Olvine."

"I can tell you do. So do I."

"Are they all about you?"

"Only that."

Chapter Three

"Tell me about the one I bought. Tell me about the turtle."

"He's a snapper. His name is 'Ulf.'"

"Well, why is he there... in the painting?"

"Why?" she asked, sitting up straight, "That's an odd question, Norval. He has to be there. It's a painting of a turtle."

"But then, the people... the rows of things?"

"Oh, they're just to give him a world. Everything and everyone needs a world to go with them. It won't be a true picture, otherwise."

Norval thought about his world, the one he fled this morning.

"And the circle of crosses?" he asked.

"More 'world,'" she sighed. "Most of the creatures keeping me company here aren't like Ulf. They don't make it for twenty years. That's how long he's lived in the pond out back. Those crosses are a family plot." Seeing her guest's frown, she patted his hand before continuing. "A graveyard is a tender thing, Norval. A ring of reminders of what used to bring joy... and continues to do so, if you allow. It's the rest of the truth about living—death. The line connecting the circle."

Norval then did what he'd never done before. Sitting with a stranger, he turned his private thoughts into words. He told Olvine about his life, of never having known his mother, his father's tyranny, Alva's terrible death. He even described the picture haunting his mind. The old woman listened, hearing everything, encouraging the telling. When he finished speaking, she made no comment... merely patted his hand again, then began preparing a meal. Her first words after the long silence were to invite him to stay the night. Enough of Norval's "old brain" remained to register rocking amazement as he calmly accepted her offer.

That evening, Olvine revealed that she, too, had suffered bitter losses in her lifetime. Her only son had also died through violence. She quietly said that even though she didn't choose to portray these things, they were clear pictures in her mind. They couldn't be wiped away, but the pain could be eased by paying full attention to the remaining wonders surrounding you.

"One can choose to do that," she whispered, more to herself than to her guest.

Silence returned as they thought their own thoughts. Olvine ended the pause by speaking in a clear, matter-of-fact voice.

"So, now what's to happen, my boy?"

"I don't know exactly," Norval answered, bringing his fingertips together, "but South Beulah, Minnesota is history now. That's the one thing I'm sure of."

"What chapter are you on... do you think?"

"Chapter?"

"I figure I'm on Chapter Eleven. There will probably be twelve chapters in my book." She paused and read through the young man's face. "I would say you are beginning Chapter Three. It's most likely the one in which you'll invent something."

Norval sat still, willing and eager for further "reading."

"I'm sure I'm right. You'll invent a thing—a way—a song—maybe even a picture. Before you can understand who lives inside there," she touched his forehead, "... before you break free of the sad old ghosts, you'll have to create something all your own."

"But I'm not an artist, Olvine. What could I invent?"

"What could you invent?" she asked as she rose and walked to the kitchen. Returning with a lighted kerosene lamp, Olvine tried to explain her idea.

"True invention requires 'seeing' with all your senses. It means allowing what you see and feel to link together and form brand new senses. That sounds odd, Norval, but it really can happen. Of course you must be looking in the right places—deep inside yourself, all around you, way out there at the horizon... all at the same time."

Norval's puzzled expression made Olvine laugh out loud.

"Poor you!" she said playfully, "Ripe for answers, and all you get is old-lady conundrums. Your brain works, lad, and your soul has muscle in it. That's enough... you'll do fine."

Norval helped make up a bed on the couch. When the pillow was in place, he remembered something that confused him.

"Your paintings are worth more than a dollar, Olvine."

"Oh yes, they are. That's why I only swap them with art-lovers, for enough pennies to keep me in turpentine and linseed."

Chapter Three

"And you manage on that?" Norval asked somewhat skeptically.

"Sure. I have my husband's small pension. Flowers, roots and tree bark give me their dyes, and I know," she looked over her shoulder, "there's enough crate boards in the shed out there to last well past Chapter Twelve."

As Norval tried to imagine *making* paint, he unfastened his buckle and stepped out of his trousers. Realizing what he'd done, he yelped and dived under the patchwork quilt. When the laughter subsided, Olvine wished him good night and carried the lamp to her bedroom.

"Do you think Old Ulf is having supper now?" The darkness seemed to amplify his words. Olvine's voice echoed slightly.

"What's that? I didn't catch it, Norval."

"I was wondering if this is perch-stalking time for Ulf."

"He dines at twilight," she replied. The light in her doorway grew brighter. "I'm sure his stomach's full and he's dreaming sweetly. You do that, too, my boy."

Norval turned on his side. "If only…"

Olvine reentered the room, set the lamp on the floor and lay her hand on the boy's shoulder. She took several deep breaths before speaking.

"Afraid of your dreams, aren't you? I remember that fear. When my son was killed, I dreaded the nights. I knew at some point I'd be sitting bolt upright in the dark, reliving the horror. One night, after this happened, I had a long discussion with myself. Why was this happening? Was there something I should be doing… some price I hadn't yet paid? What was I guilty of? I swear to you, Norval, the minute I said that word 'guilt,' I felt the pain peel right off my skull, hit the floor and bounce. Before I lay down again, I was resigned to future bad dreams. But I knew they weren't punishments, merely aftershocks."

She lifted the boy's arm from his face and set it at his side.

"Know what I think, Norval? That dreams are just plays. They are plays based on the scary things our undercover minds haven't smoothed out yet. I think you should watch the plays, give them full performance rights. If you do that, they aren't likely to harm you." She replaced the boy's arm, picked up the lamp and added, "You don't have to applaud when the curtain falls, you know."

A moment later, blackness enveloped everything.

Norval lay still, conscious of the warm nest the quilt and soft pillow provided. Play? Olvine's word seemed too short, too innocent for the horrible vision in his dream. Could it be, Norval wondered, that he might sit up in bed some night, in the middle of the scene, and deliver a good, loud "Boo?"

A small, high window was in Norval's sightline. He fixed on a star in the center panel. The star vanished and Alva took its place. She didn't appear, as she always had in previous pictures, lashed with blood, one hand clutching dead leaves and moss.

Alva was sitting under the elm tree. Lionel, her painted turtle, waddled beside her in the grass. She lifted a tear from her cheek and dropped it on Lionel's shell. It wobbled there, a tiny crystal sphere. Looking directly at Norval, she picked up the tear and threw it toward the tree-lined horizon. The arcing speck of light became a star in the center pane.

Norval studied the window. He now saw it as a little frame suspended against the night sky. He placed the images of Alva and Lionel alongside the star, then whispered to himself:

"There. There it is... my first invention."

Turning to press his face into the pillow, he shouted to an invisible proscenium arch.

"Raise the curtain! Let's get through this lousy one-acter as soon as possible."

Several deep sighs later, quiet sleep embraced him.

The Grapes of Saint Billy

1937

Deportment was the first "subject" listed on report cards at Saint Stephen's Catholic School, and Sally Rae Todd and I were the only two in our class whose column of grades was unfailingly topped with an "A." As a result, we were applauded by the elderly (our parents, Sister Francis de Paula) and pointedly ignored by classmates. Knowing that Good Deportment reflected the beauty of my soul did little to ease the suffering caused by my non-existence in the minds of the popular crowd.

Chalkboards covered three walls of the room, and along the upper edges, our souls were displayed for all to see. Each soul took the form of a stenciled bunch of grapes, below which a student's name was inscribed in the perfection of nun-lettering.

Purple grapes stood for near-sainthood. Red symbolized general goodness, undermined by lapses (whispering, chewing gum, sassy expressions). The appearance of green grapes meant things had taken place that went beyond *lapses* – that were "beneath contempt." I need hardly mention that Sally Rae Todd's and Billy Tiedman's fruit were always of the royal hue... until a certain Tuesday in springtime. My fall from grace was the doing of Roland Pitts.

Roland was big... old... sixth grade... therefore, a god. He lived two houses from me, and I was sometimes allowed to walk in his shadow on the way home. Having honed my natural gifts of good deportment to a fine art, I usually traveled in silence, letting Roland tell me things when he was in the mood. There were times when he actually invited me to speak—even to ask questions. His being the size and age he was, I asked the highest ranking question in my collection... where babies came from. He answered with a lie. Maybe a *first grader* would believe the bumps down the middle of a lady's back were zipper tracks under a secret flap of skin... but not I! When the moment seemed right, I asked the same urgent question again. This time his words were truly horrifying, so I knew they must be true. At the supper table, I studied my parents with hard eyes, trying to find signs that they were capable of such things. That night before going to bed, in the bleaching light of the bathroom, I inspected my nubbin of a penis and tried to imagine the seed-size babies packed inside it. But surely this was something green!

It was noon-hour and Roland and I were heading to our respective homes for lunch. My hero was in rare form, doing that most complimentary of things... "being honest with me." According to this god, I would not have to remain a miserable wimp all my life. I could turn into something worth noticing, but I'd have to stop being a nothing—a teacher's pet type. He, of course, could help me through the transition. It was a service older men sometimes did for younger ones. The first step, I was assured, was easier than licking ice cream.

"Come on with me to the carnival."

"Is there time?" I naively asked.

"Well, we won't be going back to school, if that's how stupid you are!"

I had barely voiced my first "but..." when he began laughing.

"Go on—get away. I should have known you're too chicken. Better run fast so Sister's little brownie won't be late."

To my horror, I felt tears rising. If he kept staring at me that way, I knew I'd never be able to halt the chugging deluge in my ducts. His eyes finally shifted to the far horizon. He reached into his jacket, produced a pack of Lucky Strikes (green in those days), shook one loose, placed it between his lips and, with a flourish that made me weak with admiration, whisked a stick-match across his rump and set the end of the cigarette aflame. The last shreds of his mortalness floated off with a wobbling smoke ring, and I knew I'd follow Roland to the ends of anywhere.

There were fields at the edge of town, about a mile from my

The Grapes of Saint Billy

home, where the carnival set up business each year. I had been to this wonderland in earlier times with my parents and remembered it as a place of laughter, painted horses and popcorn in paper cones. Today's journey was a mixture of breathless anticipation and unnamed dread. What *were* the consequences of playing hooky? With the sight of a sky-high Ferris wheel and the smell of buttered popcorn, my brain emptied itself of visions. Jingling the five heavy nickels in my pocket—a full week's milk money—I began running to keep up with Roland.

Within seconds of giving the gatekeeper my coins, I became one of the body-parts of the enormous Ferris wheel, looking down on flattened people as they moved in square dance patterns below. When the machine stopped, swinging me back and forth at the very top, my first punishment was sent. A sensation, yellowish-brown in color and of an oily consistency, began gyrating in the central loops of my belly. In an attempt to override the feeling, I scanned the horizon. Quivering in the distance, like a picture painted by God, stood St. Stephen's bell tower, which was, my conscience brutally reminded me, attached to a classroom where I… was… not! Screaming gears and a rusty coil of chain ground me back to earth. When I once again stood on the boarding platform, I was in a bad state.

Roland! Where was Roland? A fresh dose of courage was absolutely essential!

The yellow-brown swirls diminished when I saw my master leaning against a ticket stand. The slow, disgusted wagging of his head told me that my dash to the big wheel had been a mistake. He didn't, as I feared he might, stamp off and abandon me. Instead, his brows lowered and he stabbed me with a "last chance" look. A hand then slid from its pocket and, with a detonation that made me wince, it snapped its thumb and middle finger and gestured for me to follow.

We left the cluster of rides and headed down a path lined with wooden stages. Gigantic paintings on flapping canvases formed a long, high wall. The pictures were magnificent. They held scenes as raw in color and lacking in three-dimensionality as the finest comic books. One showed a man bent forward, struggling to move backward. Straining ropes stretched from the axle

South Beulah, Minnesota — Harold Huber

of a diesel truck and led to two steel hooks... one imbedded in each of the man's eyeballs. "The Amazing Otto," the picture said. Other masterpieces depicted a woman with a thick bluish beard, a skinny boy with pretzel-shaped legs biting a rooster's neck, a lady—five standard ladies in girth—in pink tights and ruffled skirt identified as "Mona—The World's FATTEST Toe-Dancer."

We stopped before a picture of a wavy-haired female wearing almost nothing. The name "Flame La Star" hovered over orange and gold tongues of fire. I turned to my guide for the proper reaction to such a bewildering sight, and what I saw doubled my amazement. There stood Roland—there stood a half-dozen other boys from St. Stephen's. William Michael Tiedman was in the presence of... being noticed by... *one of*... the popular crowd! Trying with all my might to walk sixth-gradish, I handed my nickel to a man with no teeth and entered a shadowy tent filled with folding chairs.

Flame La Star stepped into a disc of light. As the painting had promised, she was frighteningly undraped. Pinker than bubble gum, she moved about and undulated to a thin melody coming from the darkness overhead. Faint groans and whispers rose from the small audience and mixed with the eerie music. Roland bent close to me and asked, "What about those tits, huh?"

Those tits marked the first downward turn in my adventure. Was *that* a way for tits to be? Was *that* a thing for them to be called? I had learned at home to call them "a bosom," and they were formations I had always revered. My mother had them and so did all my aunts... usually encased in big flowers or polka dots. They were there to be pressed-into on birthdays, or when times were tough and one needed assurance that nothing evil would really happen. But here were these two objects... deflowered and undotted, strangely divided from each other, tipped by twirling tassels. Something was very wrong, but those I sat with seemed oblivious to the fact.

The finale of La Star's dance began when she lifted a cigarette above her head, then daintily dropped it to her feet. After sashaying around it several times, she turned her back to us and gracefully *sat on it*. Flames leapt magically from the floor and encircled her. Howls of delight burst forth when the artiste rose to her feet

The Grapes of Saint Billy

with the now-glowing cigarette clenched between the dimpled globes of her derriere.

As the St. Steve delegation wandered about in the sunlight, reliving in pantomime the marvels of La Star's artistry, I was looking for popcorn stands where I would happily deposit the last of my nickels. Roland told me to grow up. Propelled by nudges between the shoulder blades, I was moved toward another exhibit. A picture topped the entrance, but I only saw the word "Bulldog" before once again standing in a dim enclosure.

No chairs this time, only a wooden counter along the front of which we quietly stood. A gigantic man pushed through a flap on the left. His shirt was unbuttoned, showing a broad belly covered with snarls of hair. He was bald, and the grin above his chin looked painted-on. He carried something about the size of our world globe at school. Covering it was a red cloth with "Bulldog Baby" written in gold across its nubby surface. A grunt and a thud later, the mysterious object was sitting directly in front of me. I was immediately attacked by my companions, who saw my central spot at the counter as grossly unfair. A growl from the bald giant ended our scuffle, and I was allowed to remain with my face only inches from whatever was to be.

I can still see the red cloth buckling under the pressure of meaty fingers, then being swept high into the air.

The silence in the tent was so complete that I heard a black cave-sound from deep inside my head. Nothing existed but that sound and the glowing vessel in a shaft from the spotlight above.

It floated in a hands-and-knees position close to the bottom of a huge jar filled with amber liquid. The baby was the pale color of clay. A deep voice chanted but, other than "born of woman — sired of dog," I heard no words. Only my eyes were alive... nailed open and aching.

When the jar was turned to show us a different view, the little corpse wobbled and shifted, causing a delicate whirl in the sediment at the bottom. A moment later, the worst thing in the world had happened.

I was staring straight into the face of the baby. Its nose and lids were flattened to the same plane as the cheeks. An opening between each lid exposed a string-width of white. My knees folded and I rolled backward onto the damp floor. The place where I had stood was immediately filled by eager watchers.

Once past the tent flap, the gorge that had been ebbing inside me since the Ferris wheel rose again with full force. I was still on my knees when the others came out. I wanted to run and hide but my legs, like my diaphragm, had other plans. A chorus of "sissy" and "squirt" grew in volume until Roland stopped it with a mighty "Shaadup!" Apparently determined to save face before friends and to wrench some degree of success from his protege, he hauled me to my feet and wiped my polluted chin with his sleeve.

Who made you? God made me.
What is God? The maker of all things good and popular.
Who is God? Roland Pitts.
Why did Roland make you? To worship at his feet.

"Quit whining, Billy."
"But..."
"Buck up."
"But..."
"You gotta get tougher."
"Oh."
"Whaddaya wanna do next?"
I pulled my pockets inside out.
"Name it," he said, pressing a nickel into my palm.
"Popcorn," I whispered.
"Popcorn nothing!" he snapped, "We're going back there!"

Like a chewed-off leaf in an ant colony, I was jostled back toward the sideshows. The row of billboards had turned into one long scene. Gusts of wind sucked some canvases in while it billowed others out. The picture was breathing—was alive. Amazing Otto strained in the direction of Mona, whose lifted toe-shoe pointed at Flame La Star. Even though her eyes gazed leftward to the bulldog baby, she was laughing at me. The fire around her seemed to spring from the bobbing heads of the crowd. I slipped Roland's nickel into his back pocket and, in a stampede of one, ran for the exit gate.

Being as ignorant of cover-up techniques as I was inept at being popular, I slunk into the kitchen half an hour before the

The Grapes of Saint Billy

time school would end. My mother looked at me, looked at the clock, looked at me again, then continued peeling potatoes.

"You'd better change clothes and wash yourself." she said, "Father will be home soon."

Nothing could have been worse than this response from my mother. It was clear that she knew criminal acts had been committed, yet she did nothing. I needed swift justice, and she postponed the trial!

My room became an alien place. Wet from self-scrubbing, seated beside a pile of fresh duds, naked and sick to my stomach, I inspected the knee bruises from my retching-attack. I began slapping wounds, determined to inflict the cleansing pain my mother had refused me. When I added a final whack to my ridiculous penis, tears broke loose, and I remained a hiccuping wad of tension until Father opened the door to tell me supper was ready.

A forkful of potato told me that the route to my stomach was pinched off somewhere behind my tongue. Neither parent commented on my abstinence. When the silent meal ended, Mother carried the dishes to the kitchen while her husband and son sat without moving.

My father managed only a "Well, now..." before my confession erupted. Everything spilled out... my truancy, my squandered milk money, Flame La Star and her terrible—I said the word—tits. A sometimes-used expression on my father's face made it clear that that term would never again be uttered by me. It wasn't until the part about the bottled baby that his stern look softened.

The end of my confession was spoken with my forehead rocking on the tablecloth. Father's hand covered my head. Then I was pulled to the solid front of him like an undersized cello.

"I'm so sorry, Daddy."
"I know."
"I thought it would be fun."
"I know."
"Was it a sin?"
"I don't know."
"But it was bad."
"You broke a law—it was a crime."

"Then isn't it a sin, too?"

"I don't know... was it?"

Instead of demanding an answer to his puzzling question, he held me at arm's length a moment, smiled at me as a friend would, then shook out a napkin for my badly leaking face. Mother appeared carrying a peach pie and three clean plates.

Of course, my status in Sister Francis de Paula's class was never again quite the same. She continued to treat me as a human being, but her eyes narrowed slightly when I recited from the catechism. I still received A's on my report card but, for an entire week, the grapes of my immortal soul pulsated on the blackboard in eye-corroding green.

Periods of reflection through the years have made me realize that I've never quite stopped trying to make up for my second grade transgressions. Make up to whom? It's difficult to say. Sister Francis de Paula... for making her switch chalks? My parents... for spoiling the record of their perfect offspring? Sally Rae Todd... for five lonely days in saintly isolation? Roland and the popular crowd... for falling short of their standards? Well, the "who" is hazy, but the need is clear.

I just did a bit of "making up" in the supermarket yesterday. It's what reminded me of this little Morality Play from my childhood.

While waiting at the checkout counter, struggling not to focus on the loud — almost audible — and garish, ever present lineup of papparazzi-fed front pages, my eyes were slapped by a large photograph of a heavily veiled bride. She sat on a park bench holding a bull terrier on her lap. The oversize caption hollered:

WOMAN WEDS DOG IN BIZARRE CEREMONY

Tent canvases flapped in the back of my brain, and I was transported to 1937. A savage thrust from a shopping cart behind brought me back to the present, and I dutifully moved into the space that had grown between my cart and the customer ahead. A moment later, I apologized to the people in line and backed my cart out of the aisle.

When my turn finally came at the cash register, I stacked my purchases before an extremely puzzled cashier. I had gone to each checkout lane and gathered every tabloid in the store — one hun-

The Grapes of Saint Billy

dred and six of them—given the girl one-third of my paycheck (probably a year's milk money), and saved a few fellow beings from the lingering effects of Sideshow Depression.

In bed last night, I conjured up my second grade room. I placed Sister de Paula, my mother and father and Sally Rae Todd in a ring around me. I then climbed the rolling library ladder and painstaking decorated every circle and oval of my immortal, seedless soul with the most luscious purples in all of Christendom.

South Beulah, Minnesota Harold Huber

Look-to Love Song

1992

Whoo-ee! Look at me sweat! Skimpy on breath, too. It used to be I could lift up things ten times heavier than this old looking glass and barely have to blink. Them days are over, I can see. Half a dozen stops to gulp air, and I only dragged it from the bedroom to here in the kitchen. Wonder how come I feel so jittery? Well, I know why, of course. It's because I decided to finally test out a look-to and see if it really helps.

"Look-to," that's the word Sylvie made up for a good long session at her mirror. She claimed that if a person did it—did it in the proper way—even their jumpiest nerves would calm way down to near zero. Well, she was usually right about everything, so I'll give it a try.

Sylvie died in nineteen-ninety. She was eighty-seven at the end, and now I passed her by two years. Forty years before Sylvie died, almost to the day, both our children got killed in the same car accident. They was all we had, Sylvie and me. So now here sits me, stranded, the only one of our little family that's left. What in the world's a person doing, still stomping around at such an age... all alone? Nothing much, I can tell you that! Where's a person supposed to be stomping to?

Well, I'll try this look-to and see if it helps. Not that risky, I guess, except for the gooseflesh.

The first time I seen Sylvie do a look-to was just a week after we got married. Boy, she was pretty without no clothes on. I got all hammered up in one second flat. That's how it goes when you're young. I said to her, what was she trying to do to me... explode the skin off me? But that wasn't it. She wasn't one bit forward with her womanhood, like some. Sylvie believed that sitting for a long look and talk to herself — as the Lord made her — helped get down to the truth, like shucking the pod and getting down to the natural peas. I should get on with my chores and just leave her be. I banged the kitchen door, but I stayed behind the coat rack to watch.

Sylvie just sat there on the bed edge for the longest time, staring at herself in the looking glass... not moving, not doing nothing, just looking. I got nervous. When she started talking, my mind eased up. She told herself she shouldn't be fearful, not of anything... me, being a married lady, running the house... nothing. She told herself we loved each other, didn't we? That if she braced her trust against that love, things would turn out fine.

Then she got to crying, then to laughing hard. The poor girl had nothing to wipe her face or blow her nose on — naked and all — so she just sniffed and snorted and kept laughing like a loon.

I'm forever glad I watched her look-to. It made me love her double-plus. I marched right in there and hugged her 'til we was both gulping like goldfish. I always swear we got Billy cooking — our oldest — that very day.

They don't need half this many buttons on a shirt, for Lord's sakes!

It makes me laugh every time I see that spot on the glass — that place where the backing's pealed off and there's little specky clouds of nothing where you try to see. I always laugh because one day Sylvie did the funniest thing. She was standing kind of slantways, grinning and staring at herself. I asked her how come? She said if she held just right, and bull's-eyed that spot just right, her mole was gone.

That mole on her cheek was a bane to Sylvie... and she was not a vanity sort of woman. She'd say it wasn't hers — she didn't want it — how'd it get there? If we'd be heading to a dance or a wedding or anything fancy, she'd get a little overboard with her powder puff, trying to hide that blamed mole. I told her they called them "beauty marks" in the moving pictures. Didn't help. She made powder fly 'til it looked like a fog-storm in the bedroom. Then she'd come out and say — shy — she didn't look like a Jezebel,

Look-to Love Song

did she?

"Naw, maybe if you'd rouge up them cheeks," I'd say. "Soak them lips in beet juice awhile. Maybe then."

You should have heard her go to town then! Sylvie had just about the shiningest laugh that ever was.

She never came home from the hospital… room 12. All them stomach aches and dizzy spells, that was the cancer. She wasn't supposed to die when she did. The doctor said six months or maybe a year.

GOD DAMN YOU TO HELL… BASTARD CANCER!

They let me sleep most nights in a chair beside her. It was against the rules, but the night nurse turned out to be Juney Lindstrom, our neighbor's girl, who we knew since she was small as a pollywog. Who'd imagine she would sprout up to be a grown woman… and Sylvie's nurse… and a saint, at that? I'll bless her for evermore for what she did. Not the chair to sleep in so much, as the pill… that really broke the rules. She would've lost her job almost for sure if anybody would have found out. They would have had her arrested too, I'll bet… now that I think of it. But, that Juney had a heart inside her. She wasn't all charts and business and looking anxious to be off someplace while you was talking, like so many there at the hospital.

That pill would take Sylvie out of her suffering if things got too bad to bear. We never got to use it, though.

Boy, this belt's about seen its day. Overstrained, I guess, holding in the landslide.

Sylvie slipped out of this world one night while she was sleeping, while I was trying to remember how "Beautiful Dreamer" went… that last part. I remember all the words now, but I don't dare sing it.

Wouldn't you think they'd make some kind of a switch to push, and then a person's shoes would pop right off? This bending over ain't easy when a fella's pushing ninety… even lean-to'd on a kitchen chair.

Nope, Sylvie just slipped off. No last wink… no fare-thee-well. The cover just closed, as they say.

I took up talking to myself. Sylvie was right about that, too.

South Beulah, Minnesota — Harold Huber

She claimed people was *meant* to talk to themselves. How on earth else could they get things hashed out right? She said some old maid schoolteacher made up the rule that it means you're crazy... or going there. She talked to herself lots of times, even without the looking glass. She'd sing herself songs, too. Then when I caught her at it, I'd say Boo, Sylvie! She'd throw any old thing she could grab—laughing. She had the goldenest laugh that ever was.

So... here I go. Good God on Friday this chair is cold on the hinder! I should have warmed it with the coffee pot or something.

Whoa Nelly! I forgot a glass of water. Throat's so dry it's smoking. Boy, I sure am nervous.

So that's you, is it? There's more there than I pictured. How did all them lumps and hillocks sneak in on you when you wasn't looking?

That a belly... or just the Rocky Mountains? Boy, I remember when you used to be a bean pole... lanky and hair all over. Smooth as a mushroom now. White like one, too. Must come from near-ninety years of long underwear.

Are you the one she told looked like Tom Mix one day? Hard to believe.

Granite. No, that's not what I mean. Whadayacallit... marble. The whole noggin—milk-colored marble—like statuary. Boy, they could bury me heels-first and save money instead of a headstone. Except people would get to laughing. It wouldn't be fair to Sylvie. Her laying down dignified and me with my head poking out.

Well, she sure was right about this look-to business. Been sitting here I don't know how long, looking and conversing and, like she said, letting the truth come at me broadside. It's got more tonic to it than Vicks and castor oil all beat together. Not a chaff of nervousness left in the entire carcass.

I hope Sylvie was right about the other thing—what she told me before she went to sleep and slipped off. About us being together again when my turn comes. Well, we'll see.

Whoof! Water's got warm setting there. Water never is tasty from a faucet. Stinging cold in a tin cup, right out of an old handpump... that's how drinking water was meant to be. Well, warm

Look-to Love Song

or cold, Juney's pill slipped down easy as a bean, on one little swig.

Hey, Sylvie! Boo, Honey! Is that where you been hiding? I poked and hunted through every speck of this place trying to find you, hoping you didn't all-the-way leave me. I should have known you'd be in this mirror if you was anyplace. Girl, this is more like it! Things are finally getting exciting... looking up, as they say. Now, don't you budge, Sylvie.

Giddyup, little pill, time's a-wasting.

Hold on to your hat, Tom Mix... except you ain't *wearing* one!

South Beulah, Minnesota   Harold Huber

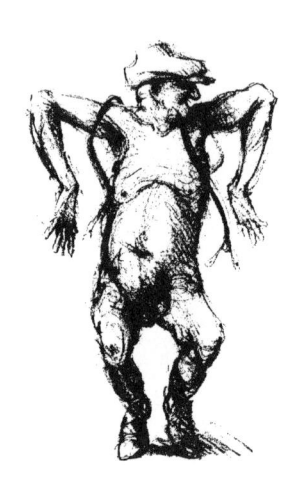

Catching Up

1967

Woodward Flower's first words were spoken at age seven when, in a well modulated voice, and with perfect enunciation, he asked his father a question.

"Is it almost over now?"

What startled Mr. Flower, even more than the puzzling question, was its clear refutation of the opinion shared by a parade of specialists that his little Woodward was *incapable* of speech. The relieved father's happiness was short-lived, however, since the boy then refused to utter another syllable for the next two years.

Woodward's second utterance took place on his ninth birthday. Flanked by his father and an aunt, blinking at an elaborate cake setting before him, Woodward asked politely, "May I have a cup of coffee?"

Throughout most of age nine, the boy spoke at sporadic intervals. Mr. Flower soon discovered his strange little boy had an adult's wide-ranging vocabulary. A series of tutors were hired, all of whom relinquished their positions within weeks, each claiming the lad was ineducable. His vocabulary notwithstanding, he seemed unable to comprehend abstractions or make deductions. He could, they agreed, repeat almost anything he'd ever heard, but they doubted he understood what most of it meant. Therefore, the father's amazement was great when, on Woodward's fifteenth birthday, he voiced a lengthy and complex theory.

"The Wilburns' lawn has not been cut for two weeks. There is a large pile of newspapers beside the front steps. A light goes on in a second-floor window at night. Someone has murdered the Wilburns and is staying in their house."

Woodward's conclusion proved correct. The next week, an escaped convict was returned to Illinois, the neighboring couple was buried and the house was sold. When Mr. Flower asked his son what it was that made him suspect murder, the boy's calm reply was that the situation was identical to a Perry Mason show in 1966.

Finding that his son was fully capable of reasoning, he called a friend on the school board and asked for help in slipping Woodward into the public school system. A high school equivalency test was arranged. The test revealed a serious problem. Woodward neither read nor wrote, implying he should enter school as a first grader. But verbal examinations showed, in terms of accumulated information and comprehension, he ranked well above senior high school level. It was decided a tutor once again be employed.

Lydia Fields was engaged to teach Woodward his ABCs. She was a recent speech graduate who had specialized in dealing with learning disabilities. She welcomed the part-time job as a way of supporting an ailing, widowed mother and an addiction to blue movies.

When Mr. Flower introduced Lydia to her pupil, Woodward reacted in an unexpected way. He blushed, covered his eyes and backed out of the room. This behavior was something new to Mr. Flower. His son usually met all situations, novel or familiar, with the same unresponsive, disquieting calm. Upon further reflection, however, his boy's peculiar reaction began to make sense. With the exception of Amy, Mr. Flower's sister, all Woodward's "sitters" or would-be companions through the years had been professional men, counselors and therapists. The man realized that, other than Aunt Amy, Miss Fields was the first non-televised female to enter the house since the lad's mother died when he was two.

Daily lessons were inaugurated. Lydia arrived at noon, and after the first hour, when Mr. Flower returned to his office, student and teacher were left alone to pursue their work at the large blackboard leaning against a breakfront in the sun room. Lydia attacked her task with fervor. The boy seemed pleasant enough, even though he never initiated a single exchange... only re-

Catching Up

sponded to questions or directives to speak. She was astonished at his speed in mastering every segment of their work. She had to invent her own program, since her training had not prepared her to deal with a student who understood everything as quickly as it was explained.

By the second week, Woodward's reading was virtually flawless, so they concentrated on the confusing aspects of English spellings. She discovered that if she spelled a word aloud, Woodward never forgot it. She also gradually became aware of something new and unexpected in his behavior. During lessons, the boy's gaze often anchored on her chest, or slowly traveled along her body's contours. Lydia saw, in these moments, a look of confusion and something resembling fright... brief, flickering interruptions in his otherwise cool, steady focus. Without warning, the odd interlude would end, and Miss Fields was once more feeding information into her passive learner.

One day Woodward surprised his teacher by being the first to speak. He told her he liked to draw pictures, that he drew them at night in his room. He wished he had a book about the human body. With his seemingly boundless capacities in mind, and believing he might be impressed by its mighty girth, Lydia bought a paperback copy of *Gray's Anatomy* and presented it to Woodward at the beginning of their next class. As she listed homophones on the chalkboard, the boy paged through his gift. When Lydia finished the list and turned, he threw the book at the French windows, then hid his face. Thinking he was ill, Lydia went to Woodward and lifted his head. He slowly raised his hands and placed them on her breasts. He rose and pressed his face into her bosom. They stood without moving. Several minutes later, the young woman put her arm around his shoulders and spoke quietly.

"Show me the drawings."

His room contained furniture, but no decorations of any kind. Nails in the walls suggested things had once been otherwise. Woodward spread a dozen sheets of paper over the bed. Each page portrayed a standing, genderless figure drawn with a single outline. It suddenly struck Lydia that the book she'd chosen must have been a terrible disappointment to Woodward. His eyes remained on the drawings as she gently unbuttoned his shirt, removed his clothing, then her own. With the white pages crackling beneath them, Miss Fields brought her student through his second lesson of the day.

That evening Lydia returned and told Mr. Flower that his son could now read and write. Looking at the boy's back as he stood in his habitual place at the French doors, staring at the tree-lined horizon beyond the garden, she added, "I've taught him what I think he needs to know. He's outstanding in every area."

The gratified father made out a check, and Miss Fields departed to find a more conventional outlet for her training.

When the door closed behind Miss Fields, Mr. Flower patted his son's back and said, "Well, now we'll have to hunt up something new for you to learn." Woodward's eyelids began to flutter rapidly, and for an entire month, he was mute. Desperate for help, Mr. Flower summoned his sister.

Aunt Amy was ready with a solution. She reminded her brother that the boy had been born and bred in the townhouse.

"What he needs is to be introduced to nature... the reality of the land rather than televised snippets of it."

A trip was quickly arranged for seven days in the Adirondacks at a hideaway cabin belonging to one of The Flower Company's vice-presidents.

Woodward and his aunt spent a week in an old cottage built at a cliff-edge overlooking a spectacular vista. Miss Flower congratulated herself when, at the end of the first day, her nephew began speaking again. She indulged in her hefty repertoire of poetic phrases during their walks. She led him through wooded hills and into small valleys. Being a botany enthusiast, Aunt Amy pointed out and named countless varieties of ferns and mosses. Her barely disguised quizzes in the evenings convinced her the boy had learned them all. She searched his features for signs of delight, but, as was always true with Woodward, he viewed the wonders surrounding them with no readable facial expression.

On their last evening, nephew and aunt stood at the stony precipice looking at the blood-blazing western sky. Without turning his head, Woodward asked, "Is it just about over?"

"Our trip?" Amy took his hand and squeezed. "Oh,

Catching Up

Woodward... I thought you were enjoying it."

The boy shook his head, indicating that was not what he'd meant.

"Is there anything left... that I have to learn?"

Thinking she'd grasped his line of thought, Aunt Amy began to chuckle.

"Well, dear, you can read and you can write, and it seems to me you *know* just about everything! And now you've spent time out here—seen and felt the scale and grandeur of Nature—witnessed the natural order of things." She cleared her throat several times, searching for a fittingly grand conclusion for her thought. "I would say a logical next step would be to become part of that order, and to find you something... to do." Seeing his brows lower, she quickly added, "... but, of course, there's plenty of time for that. But someday, my boy, you'll find a sweetheart, and then..."

Woodward pulled his hand from hers and once again shook his head. Amy tried to read her nephew's frowning profile. Then her eyes followed his steady gaze to the narrowing band of red at the horizon. After a long silence, the elderly woman sighed and spoke barely above a whisper.

"And then, of course... there's God."

Woodward turned to face his aunt. "Where?" he asked. "Where is God?"

"Where?" Amy repeated, her voice shaking slightly. "Why, He's everywhere."

"Down there?" He gestured toward the darkening ravine at the brink of which they stood.

The old woman stepped back from the cliff's edge, nodding her head.

The boy slowly and carefully pivoted, with both arms fully extended.

"Is God there?—and there?—and there?"

Aunt Amy, feeling the chill of the oncoming night air, shivered. "Yes... yes, of course, dear."

Woodward pointed to the remaining bright thread of magenta sky and asked, "There, too?"

"My darling boy..."

Amy's words caught in her throat. She had never before seen

~ 69 ~

South Beulah, Minnesota — Harold Huber

such an expression on her nephew's face. It was a look of genuine joy. So great was her astonishment that she was unable to speak—even to move—as Woodward stepped into God's space beyond the escarpment and, with arms opened like moth wings, plunged into the velvety blackness below.

Gerald and Juliet

1955

Gramma makes everybody crazy except me and Leander. Leander is not very smart, so I'm the one who has to get Gram out of trouble when she gets into it, which is all the time, even more than me. Summer vacation is worst for trouble. That's because it gets hot, and my parents and my sister Fern get cranky when they sweat.

I am getting pretty good at watching out for Gramma, but it took me a long time to spot the dangerous stuff, the stuff that makes my father and mother talk to her like she was a dumber mutt than Leander. They don't realize she gets insulted when they talk that way. It's almost like they forgot that Gramma is my own mother's very own mother! And what does she do that is so awful? Maybe because she likes to play again, after so many years of having to be a grown-up.

Here's one of Gramma's dangerous games. When I hear she's starting to play it, I have to get her to switch. That is not an easy thing to do because Gram *knows* what she knows and *likes* what she likes and *does* what she does. That is what she says a hundred times a day. I think it makes her sound just like a president of the United States, but everybody—even Fern—looks at her grumpy every time she says it.

The game only has one rule. Gramma says something that is all wrong and then waits for people to get crazy from it. Once, while we were eating supper, she said to my mother, "I named you Harmon, not Thelka." You should have seen my mother then. She looked just like when Leander licks her right on the mouth. She said Harmon was "brother's" name and that Gramma was

South Beulah, Minnesota Harold Huber

mixed up again. Gram slapped the table and said she ought to know what she named her own children! Me and Gramma both got in a laughing fit, but mother didn't think it was even a little bit funny. My mother didn't used to be so grumpy when I was little, but now that I am seven and Gramma is eighty-eight, she can act just like the wicked witch in *The Wizard of Oz*. Gram says Mother is getting senile. It's too bad.

The safest time for fun is when me and Gramma run races. She makes me do it backward, but she runs the regular way. When I said, "But Gram, you always win that way," she said, "Well *sure*... that's the rule." One thing in our games is that we never break the rules, no matter what. But they have to be good ones or it's no fun to play. Whoever makes up the game gets to make up the rules for it. Gramma is so smart she can think up brand new rules every time we play an old game. I hope I am almost a genius when I get eighty-eight.

But our best game of all is The Play Game. Nobody has to win that one, and Gram says that's what makes it so great. These are the rules. After we finish eating, Gramma says she has to take a nap. Then I say I have to, too. This is the favorite thing my mother and father like to hear. In a little while, Gram taps on my door and we head up to the attic... just where we are not allowed to play! Getting up there isn't easy because the steps make loud squeaks that sound like Leander barking. We have to walk on the edge of the steps and hold on to each other over the middle. Once we're up and get the inside door closed, it's okay and we are safe.

There are three big boxes up there and we get our costumes for the plays out of them. When Gramma chooses, she for sure picks the white veil. I pick capes and leather boots and always the sword with sparkles on the holder. We do not make shows of "Little Red Riding Hood" and other ordinary stories. We only do grown-up plays. I am usually Superman and Gramma is Gloria Swanson. They are our favorites. Gloria Swanson was best for acting when Gramma went to the movies.

One story we do all the time is "Romeo and Juliet." I am Romeo, the boy, and she is Juliet, the girl. I marry Gramma and we live in a balcony. Then we kill ourselves. It's so much fun! When we can sneak Leander up, it's even better. Leander is

Gerald and Juliet

Gramma's dog and came along when she moved to our house. That was when I was little and before I got my memory. Daddy doesn't like Leander, but Mother says he's okay when he behaves. Anyway, when Leander is in the play, he gets a beanie tied on his head so he will look like a monk... like they have in the Catholics. Then he marries me to Gram and we live happily ever after until it's time to kill ourselves.

My gramma could win the Academy Awards if she would only be on television. She can make you believe anything in a play, even when she says "thou" and "thee" and "art." That's how you say "you" and "me" and "are" in Gloria Swanson talk... like, "Art thou getting hungry, Gerald?" It is something you have to practice.

When Juliet says she cannot live anymore without her beloved, Gramma makes real tears come out. Sometimes she does it for the longest time, and then I want to cry, too. We can even quit realizing it is just a play. Yesterday, when I went to her room to see if she wanted to race me, she said who was I? I said, "Gramma... I'm Gerald." She said Gerald was dead — that Gerald was her father. I started to get scared so I said, "I art Romeo, my fair Juliet." Then she blinked hard and then she hugged me. That's how I knew she was playing the game. See what I mean about Academy Awards?

I can't see why my gramma is always the one who gets yelled at worst, because I do everything she does. When Daddy gets mad, he always says the same thing. We should act our age. But the thing I want to know is how does he know how to act eighty-eight? He must have been seven once, even if it's like he can't remember it, but he couldn't have been eighty-eight yet.

Last night, Gramma got sick, and now everybody is being nice to her when she has to stay in bed all the time... even Fern. I don't like it when it's not my turn to sit with Gramma. I said I wanted to take all the turns, but Mother said to behave. I am the only one Gram really wants there. I think it's because everybody else is senile.

Gramma was crying when I went for my turn, but when she saw I brought the white veil so she could be Juliet, she almost got well again. I snuck the big comb from the bathroom and combed out all her white hair around on the pillow. It was so soft and shiny. She looked like our Christmas star on the tree, with Juliet's face in the middle. She liked when I told her she looked that way. She told me, "Thou art my love forever." When my father came in for his turn, I quick hid the veil under her pillow.

This morning Gramma is dead. She died last night when she couldn't even tell me she was going to do it. Gramma is dead and I hate everybody. I locked me in the bathroom, but my father said I had to come out no matter how bad I felt. Now I don't know what to do.

When the men came to put Gramma in the black car that takes you to heaven, my mother said the worst thing I ever heard her say. She said it was a blessing that Gram is dead. Fern said it too — that old ladies like her are too old to keep living. I was going to get the sword from our play in the attic and kill Fern, but I didn't. I thought of how bad Gramma felt when people got hurt on television, and I didn't want her watching from up in the sky, feeling sad. Leander cried all day in the back yard. That is enough people crying who I love.

I know something that would make them sorry they blessed Gramma dying at me... if I ran away and was an opera singer, or a Republican. That is who they don't like the most. But I won't do that either. Gramma would say "bad rules," not playing fair. She told me good rules make you feel happy, like laughing when the game is done. She could always think of new good ones, no matter what. I wish I could.

I wonder if I could teach my mother and father how to play some of our games? They might like to know how to have fun again, even if they are grown-ups. Leander could help me. We would have to go slow at first and kind of sneak it in on them. If Mother learned the rules first, then she could help us show Daddy how. They could practice when there's nothing good on TV. We better just skip Fern.

That is exactly what I'll do! Gramma will like it.

If I squint my eyes and jiggle them a little, I can see her like in a Gloria Swanson movie, only with colors in it. Gramma is sitting on the edge of her balcony in heaven, and there are Christmas stars all around her. She is wearing her long white Juliet veil. She

Gerald and Juliet

is wiggling her toes and winking and waving her hand. She is calling down to me, "What for art thou waiting for, Romeo?"

South Beulah, Minnesota   Harold Huber

The Pinky Quest

1937, 1978

My cousin makes sure I don't completely lose touch with the small town in which she and I grew up, and where she still lives. Last month's note from her was taped to a full page of the South Beulah Weekly. An item in the "We Have Lost" column was circled in red ink:

> Sarah Elisabeth Munro, former resident of our city, was found dead last Wednesday at Adwell's Rooming House in St. Paul. Miss Munro left no known family.

I was stumped as to why Carole had sent this odd and empty obituary. I couldn't recall a single Sarah-anybody from the old days. The back side of her note solved the mystery.

"P.S. I thought you'd want to know about Pinky."

Pin-kee! The two syllables catapulted my brain back to 1937. She lived downtown, on Pink Street. My cousin and I lived with our parents a half-block away on busy River Avenue, in the rear quarters of the OK Inn. We often heard customers say she was the only "professional" in town, but, according to our observations, she had no profession, unless window shopping was a job. Grown-ups had many names for her, but the most used one was "Pink Street Lady." To Carole and me she was just Pinky.

Her hair was the color of corn-candy and had the texture and kinky brilliance of copper scouring pads fresh out of the box. This feature, along with gaudy silken dresses and shoes having ice picks for heels, made her the most beautiful human being walking the tavern fronts on River Avenue. When asked why other ladies didn't copy the way she looked, our mothers, in identical pantomimes, smoothed their rounded apron bibs and told us to "Go play!" Eventually convinced that no grown-up would supply the needed information, Carole and I launched a sleuthing campaign that lasted most of the summer.

Because Carole was the best speller and could write fast, She carried the "BIG 5" tablets on our forays. I was Pencil Man. When spotting Pinky, we'd duck into doorways, write down what she was wearing, then follow her until something noteworthy took place. We soon discovered the fallacy of an earlier belief: that no one ever spoke to her. Occasionally a man stopped beside her to study the same window display. They didn't look at each other, but we saw their lips moving. When he left, Pinky would open her purse and write something in a tiny book. These side-by-side encounters supplied the only hint of "plot" in our investigative reports.

Our first really satisfying discovery was that Pinky lived at the Rodeo Bar Hotel. One day, summoning all our courage, we boldly entered the bar. We were immediately ushered out by a gigantic one-armed man wearing a cowboy hat. His parting words convinced us that we had better resume our covert methods. The glassed-in entryway of Grant's Furniture became our waiting station.

Being stationed at Grant's was not a hardship. The pictures displayed in its large windows were among the few objects capable of taking our minds off Pinky. They were not ordinary pictures—four or five inches deep—like medicine cabinets. The inner frames were lined with shelves on which stood miniature candles, vases of dried flowers and the like. Inspirational postcards graced the recesses. While blinking in the glow of these art treasures, Pinky all but evaporated from our minds. But on first glimpse of our walking rainbow, we were back on the job.

By midsummer, our quest was in need of a transfusion. We decided to act on a longstanding plan. After church one Sunday, with gift-filled paper bags in hand, Carole and I climbed the rusty fire escape ladder behind the Rodeo Bar Hotel. At the fourth floor window (large windows served as exit portals to the fire escape), our trembling eyes collided with the long-lashed orbs of our

The Pinky Quest

quarry. The grimey pane slid upwards. Her greeting had a song in it.

"Come on in, dearies. Whatever took you so long?"

In only seconds, our nervous tremors had shaken loose and flown out the open window. Pinky was as pleasant and perfect as she looked. She served hot cocoa while telling wonderful stories about drum majorettes and of having reigned as MISS WILMET HIGH SCHOOL for an entire year.

She oohed and smacked her lips over the assorted candy bars we'd "borrowed" from the reachable display racks at the OK Inn, and in return for the gifts, Pinky taught us.

We learned that bright colors improved your health, that Carole's feet were almost big enough for high heels, that life was all peaks and craters, that liquor and cigarettes shrunk the brain, and that bad dreams lost their nasty fizz if you made up songs about them. We also learned there was one adult in the world who didn't answer a single question with "Go play!" Before descending the fire escape, we promised Pinky we would not speak to her on River Avenue, but that we would—Oh Boy! Would we!—come again for more Sunday visits.

I never saw Pinky again. When Carole and I got home, our parents were waiting. They said nothing about jail or reform school. Their words were much worse. Two terrible sentences. "We're selling the OK Inn," and "We won't be living together from now on." Before summer ended, my cousin had moved up on the hill, to be closer to Uncle's new job. My parents and I moved here, five hundred miles away. In the following decades, I did not return to South Beulah.

In what I thought of as "The Play of Harry's Grown-up Life," Pinky became a bit player, a cartoon figure that I conjured up at parties. I always won at the tales-of-childhood contests that were so popular with my crowd. Who else could claim they hung around prostitutes at age seven? That's about where things stood in April. Then Carole's note and newspaper fell through my mail slot.

When the time came for my vacation, I decided forty years was long enough. I called my cousin, and she agreed to pick me up when my train arrived at Midway Terminal. Instead of driving directly to her home, we stopped downtown. The street signs claimed we were on the corner of Pink and River, but they lied. The low strip of taverns and storefronts was gone, office buildings and parking structures denied their ever having been there. What should have been the alley behind the Rodeo Bar Hotel was a smooth driveway leading to Beulah Nursing Home. Carole nudged me toward the entrance.

An old man sat dozing in the day room. He wore a cowboy hat and his left arm ended at the elbow. Carole nudged his shoulder.

"Huh? Oh, it's you," he said, grunting to a more upright position, "and this must be that cousin of yours. You're Harry I bet."

His handshake was surprisingly strong. He said I should call him Tex.

"Your cousin here says you want to know about Sarah Elizabeth. Glad to oblige. Sit." He pointed to nearby chairs. "Put your feet up if you wanna. They don't care around here.

"Sarah Elizabeth was the nicest person ever got born. She got a real kick outta the both of you... called you her 'baby bloodhounds.' She came out of Chicago with her new-married husband back in '16. He got blowed up in World War One and she had to go to hustling to feed herself. Must've been about fifty when you scallawags was sniffing her trail.

"Sarah Elizabeth was pure lady. You know... refined. Nobody could talk dirty to her. If they did, their name got scratched off her book. No name ever got back on either, once her pencil dragged across it. Everybody liked her... respected her. Of course, people took things for what they was back then. Cheering up gents was her job, plain and simple. Some worked at the stockyards, some tended bar, some did whatever. Sarah Elizabeth worked Room Eleven. Everybody was happy."

Tex fished in his shirt pocket, offered each of us a fuzz-fringed peppermint and continued his narration.

"Yup, she worked all night, but she got up early next day. She spent mornings reading books and making all them pictures. They sold them over at Grant's. She was a genuine artist. Well, wrinkles and arthritis put the brakes on her working days. After a couple years she finally pulled up stakes and took a room in St. Paul. I

The Pinky Quest

kept meaning to call her up one day, but... well, I was always shy of her."

The old man mumbled and counted on his fingers.

"She must've been near ninety when she passed. Makes you think, don't it?"

His next words were whispered—spoken to his fingertips.

"Don't suppose she'll get a headstone. You know, a monument."

He paused again, then slid far away to some private realm. Taking his silence as a sign that we should leave, Carole and I stood up. Tex blinked back to the present and grabbed my sleeve.

"Hold on, don't go! I got presents... from Sarah Elizabeth." He lifted the blanket from his lap, revealing two cardboard boxes braced between his knees. "Came near throwing 'em a hundred times. Glad I didn't now. After you came to see me," he winked at Carole, "I dug 'em out of my box. See? 'Carole' on this one, 'Harry' on that. She gave them to me to give to you if I ever caught sight of you again. Know what she told me? That you was the only two little children she ever talked to in twenty years. Think of that... only two in twenty years. Sarah felt real bad when you didn't come back. Her handwriting's pretty, ain't it?"

Carole's parcel contained a prom dance card and a small scrapbook filled with catalogue cut-outs of children in old-time fancy clothes. Lipstick prints on some of the images had stained adjoining pages. My gift hangs on a narrow wall in my apartment. The frame is deeper than any of those we gasped over in Grant's windows.

In the central panel of a triptych, Abe Lincoln looks down at gothic letters spelling out the first lines of the Gettysburg address. To the left is a sepia photograph of a bearded man and a smiling, seated woman across whose lace-covered knees is written, "Ma and Pa." The opposite photo shows a young man in a doughboy uniform. His eyes pierce the filmy grayness, and one finger points directly at the viewer. His lips are puckered for a mighty kiss. Bold letters in blue ink spell out "Joe."

The day I hung Pinky's bequest on the wall, my conscience launched its first assault. Each time I passed the picture, I felt more ashamed of having turned my childhood heroine into a party joke. I began searching for ways to... to what? To erase my treachery? To clear Pinky's name with the party crowd? I realized whatever I said to them would be heard as Part Two of an old joke. I also realized Pinky had no need for earthly reparations, and that, were she somehow given the choice, she would forgive her baby bloodhound rather than drag a pencil through his name. Still, I needed to do something in order to forgive myself. Last week, the answer came to me. It was a small and simple something.

I glued a strip of paper to the bottom of Pinky's obituary. After the line, "...left no known family," I carefully printed these words:

> *but she is mourned by those she comforted, and joyously remembered by three special loved ones."*

Then, having removed the picture's backing, I fastened my small document below the pale icons inside and quickly resealed the panel before the last threads of air from decades past could escape.

In my letter to Carole, I asked that she greet Tex for me and give him the photograph I had enclosed. The picture will please him. I know it will make his old heart happy to see — with his very own eyes — that Sarah Elizabeth does have a proper and beautiful monument.

Willy's Fall

1980

Willy Leonards is three weeks older than me, but we're both thirteen. He has been my best friend since we were kids. When we were ten, we made up a whole complete language and Willy even made a dictionary for it. He taught me to ice skate and he learned roller from me. We used to have code words for just about everything important. That's because we both planned to join the FBI when we got older. Typical kidstuff! We're still best friends after all these years, but exactly why this is true, I couldn't tell you. I mean, there's things you have to hate about him.

He doesn't smoke, drink beer, swear or knock up women. Roland Dufort is the one who pointed these things out. He says Willy isn't human—doesn't do the normal, healthy things an eighth-grade man does. Roland ought to know... he does them all the time. He tells us about each one the next day, after he's done it—especially when he's knocked up a woman. He says we're all wimps... still only choking the old turkey. Well, I don't know... I guess the reason I like Willy best is that when he talks to you, you can *tell* he's your friend. Roland *says* we're all his buddies, but it doesn't quite feel like he's your friend exactly. I guess when you've been around as much as Roland, you get past that kind of stuff. You can't help but admire the guy.

Roland and Willy are deadly enemies, which is surprising when you realize that Willy doesn't even act afraid. He'll just come right out and say Roland stinks—right out where everybody can hear it. The surprising part is that Roland could beat Willy's ass off if he decided to. That's what he says all the time. "I could beat that fucker's ass off if I felt like it. Only I don't feel like it. I might

South Beulah, Minnesota   Harold Huber

kill the sissy fucker." Roland walks away whenever Willy comes by. I guess he doesn't want to go to jail for murder. His father was in jail two years for robbing the liquor store. Roland says his dad's a wimp for getting caught. He says all you have to do is never take more than one beer at a time, and they'll never catch you. He's right, too. Last Saturday, we had a blast at Roland's garage — thirteen bottles of "hand-picked" brew. Roland drank the most, naturally; and boy, did he have a hangover the next day, he told us.

    Willy wasn't at the blast, but he knew about it. That's another thing about Willy, he never rats on anybody. Well, he did once in sixth grade. Willy told Hog-face Hanson on Roland, right when the peephole he was digging out between the boys' and girls' toilets was already almost all the way through. Everybody was sure mad at Willy... me too. But I forgave him. He didn't know any better. He's dumb in a couple of ways, even though he's the smartest person in our grade. For instance, when Roland can't answer a question in class, Willy always puts his hand up and gives the right answer. He must not realize that that makes Roland mad enough to kill him. But like I say, Willy gets these dumb streaks — or else he wants to get his ass beat off. At least Willy doesn't rat on him anymore. That's a relief.

    Right now, I'm pretty worried about Willy... Willy and me, I mean. Maybe we might not be able to stay best friends anymore. That's because Roland says Willy's a fag. He's been telling everyone that for over a week. Wow... did I see red when I heard that! I couldn't believe such a thing about Willy. Finally, I just couldn't stand it anymore, so I asked Willy right out. I said, "Are you a fag, Willy?" I expected him to really get mad, but instead he said — what's that? I said, "a fag... you know, a guy that likes boys." Willy said *I* liked boys, didn't I? He said all the guys liked boys — that they didn't hang around with *girls,* did they? Well, that was Willy being stupid again. I told him, no... it's when you love them... want to knock them up. That's the hardest I ever heard Willy laugh. I kept asking him was it true. But the more I asked, the more Willy laughed. I told him Roland says he could prove it... if he wanted to. Willy laughed so hard then that he had to fall

Willy's Fall

on the ground and hold his sides.

So now, here I am. I still don't know if it's true. I'm really getting worried. Everybody knows that being a fag is worse than being a psycho. I don't know what to do.

This afternoon, Roland is going to show a movie in his garage. He says it's real hot! It's his father's movie and he always keeps it hidden; but Roland found it and he's going to show it to us at three-thirty. He says the woman in it's got knockers that stick way out to *here*. He says she lets the guy in the movie knock her right up and that she screams, but says she loves it. He says it's all there — with everything showing! He says we're going to have a beat-off contest when it's over. He says to ask Willy to come — that if he isn't a fag, he'll do it.

I just got back from Willy's house. I had to ask him one more time… was he a fag? Willy shut his eyes and said I shouldn't ask him that again. So I told him about Roland's movie and contest. I explained that Roland said for sure he was a fag if he didn't come. That is when Willy told his first-ever lie to me. He said there was this thing he never meant to tell, but *now* he would. He said that last week, before school started, Roland stopped him in the empty lot past the swimming pool. He said Roland tried to touch him on the crotch — that he begged Willy that they should knock each other up. I couldn't believe my ears. How could a person tell such a lie about a guy like Roland? Willy must have thought I was born yesterday. I finally said to him, "Look! Are you coming to the show… or not?" He just looked at me for awhile and then said, "No."

After Willy said that, he kept staring at me. He wasn't crying exactly, but there were tears wobbling on his eyes. I turned around fast and started walking home. I wanted to kill myself. When I got far enough away, I started crying. I couldn't help it… just like some sissy girl!

It is eleven minutes… almost twelve minutes after three. It's all up to Willy now. If he doesn't show up when the movie starts, well… then I guess that's it. I'll just dump him… the lousy fag.

South Beulah, Minnesota Harold Huber

Twenty-Fifth Circle

1976

Lena sat in the day room watching her fellow residents breathe, remembering the day she danced for Isadora Duncan. She was seventeen in 1923, when Miss Duncan wafted into South Beulah to conduct an "Isadora Springtime." When the festive day ended, Lena was drawn aside and told by the ethereal dancer that she had "the gift." In the following sixty years, Lena never received a more stirring compliment.

Lena's eyes became filled with collapsed figures in wheelchairs. To empty them, she turned to the curtainless picture windows. The vista was unexciting, but it was *out there,* and she often thought that if she could once again get to such a wonderful place, the first thing she would do is scrub away the grimy outer surface of the glass. Myra was lucky. She couldn't see all the shoddy housekeeping. Lena immediately rebuked herself, knowing the unutterable joy it would bring her friend to be able to see the soiled layers, or even the windows. Myra, who was legally blind, had been at the home for eleven years—five years longer than Lena.

The two women spent most evenings together, Lena reading aloud from one of the books on her narrow shelf of treasures. This evening ritual constituted the high point of their shared life at the nursing home. Sometimes they simply sat together and talked, swapping stories about life, making up not-always-kind limericks about "The Endless Re-runs," a term they coined for many of their fellow residents. When either woman greeted the other as "Knut" or "Gipper," it was the signal that a pep talk was needed, that the hunching gray Courage-Killer was stalking.

"It's old Bjornson tonight," Lena said, wheeling into Myra's room.

Lena read for over an hour and, as frequently happened, the recital ended with Myra quietly weeping. Lena no longer commented on her friend's tears. She knew their cause and understood no words were called for. Myra had often said that she would manage the days well enough, if only she could see a beautiful page of print once again. Myra found Lena's hand, and in a few minutes, the tears were rhymed out of existence. The medium for their lifted spirits was the self-proclaimed grande dame of the home, Neva Felch. Having used up "squelch," "welch," and "belch," they began inventing new words. As the syllables became sillier, their laughter became louder, until it was stopped abruptly by a cry from the next room. A new patient was being moved in and things were apparently not going well. Aware that the time for laughter had ended, the friends parted with a goodnight kiss.

That night, in the darkness of her room, Lena listened to an old man's thin voice echoing in the hallway. "Don't turn out the light, Mommy. I'm scared, Mommy."

Lena made her customary trip to the day room at midmorning. The rain-cloud sky, trapped in the picture window, seemed a fitting background for the wheelchair islands floating on their spokes in the huge space. There sat Donna, whose left side looked dead, even when the right was animated. There was vain Neva, waving breezes across her face and too-auburn curls with what she called her "genuine Jay-pan fan." One of Mr. Arneson's fingers lifted and fell on his lap, as his filmy eyes aimed at a pillar. Nurse Wilson, with her gaudy brand of energy, split through the quiet scene, pushing a wheelchair in Lena's direction. In it was the man whom they had heard in the night. His slender bones were curved into the cushions, and a sling across his chest kept him from slumping forward.

"Lena, this is Charles Jensen," Miss Wilson said.

Lena studied her fragile neighbor. His white hair had been combed back, but several locks fell onto his forehead. His eyes were open and innocent, and pinned on Lena. Calling her "Mommy," he told her that he hadn't forgotten his prayers. When

Twenty-Fifth Circle

he began sobbing, she moved close and took his hands, assuring the frightened man that he was safe, that there was nothing to fear. Lena realized she was lying to the old man, that there was plenty to fear. But, she reminded herself, some lies make life bearable.

On leaving the day room, she saw a doctor and two nurses conferring outside Myra's door. "What is it?" Lena asked. They waved her away impatiently and continued their discussion. She caught sight of Myra's pale feet on the bed — motionless — tipped from each other like an open clamshell. Lena pushed with both hands, spun into her own room and slammed the door. She felt the skin on her face tighten. She thought of frost overtaking a winter window. For a moment, her eyes paused at "Dante" on the spine of a tilted book on her shelf. "Twenty-four circles in *that* hell," her brain whispered. Both eyes were closed when the quiet knock sounded and the door opened a crack.

"I'm so sorry," Miss Wilson's voice shook as she spoke. "Myra is gone." She was puzzled by Lena's halting, toneless response.

"Yes... thank you... twenty-*five* in this one."

Lena remained in her bed. She did nothing, resisted all attempts by the staff to get her up and about. She studied a stain of concentric rings on the ceiling, tracing the isobaric bands with her eyes, refusing to let her mind form thoughts. The nurses fed her as they would an infant, coaxing and scolding.

Several mornings later, when the sun slashed through the window's glass and split her room diagonally, Lena allowed her focus to leave the overhead circles and follow the beam to a spot on her bookshelf. She struggled into the wheelchair, lifted Bjornson from its row and went to Charles Jensen's room. He smiled and began sucking his thumb when she entered. Lena flipped pages to a bookmark and started reading aloud at the place she'd stopped a week earlier.

Lena tended to him whenever the nurses allowed. She read to him, sang songs and played finger games with him. He became her sole interest... her occupation. At staff meetings, Lena was often discussed. Minor conflicts arose as to the appropriate name for the old woman's abrupt recovery from her friend's death. Miss Wilson eagerly offered, "Second motherhood?"

South Beulah, Minnesota Harold Huber

Charles became calmer under his new mother's ministerings. When he took to sleeping for longer periods, Lena returned sporadically for brief visits to the limbo stillness of the day room. At these times, she sat quietly in a corner watching others watching her.

It was in this setting that Theodore Enger made his appearance. He had been admitted during Lena's hiatus. Whenever she was present, he positioned his wheelchair near Lena's. She turned away at his early advances, but eventually his calm manner and cheerful monologues won her over. By the time she spoke her first words to him, she knew much of his history—his loves and interests. One bright afternoon, when Theodore once again spoke of his years as a dance band pianist, Lena broke her silence.

"Play for us on talent night."

"I might just," he chuckled, cracking his knuckles. "Nothing wrong with my fingers, I guess. Tell you what—I'll do it if you join me." He winked at Lena and slapped his knee. "I'll play—you'll sing."

"Good heavens!" Lena gasped, "I would as soon do that as… well, I don't know what!"

"I'll play—you'll sing," he repeated with finality.

"You are a madman," she laughed, swatting at his dramatically raised hand. "You are a pianist, Theodore. *Play* the piano! It's such a simple concept."

"No musical talents at all?" he asked in a defeated tone.

"Well… one time…"

"What?" Theodore asked, lurching forward in his chair.

"It was so long ago."

"What? What?" he demanded.

"Well, when I was a girl, I danced for Isadora Duncan," she said.

"Isadora? Whoo-ee!" he yelled, spinning his chair in a full circle. "Okay… that's it. I'll play and you dance. It's settled."

Had the madman, by any chance, noticed that the lady was in a wheelchair? Of course the madman had, but what did that have to do with anything? What then, did the madman think, was the lady to use for *legs*? Did the lady really believe that anyone remembered what Isadora did with her *legs*? Wasn't it those graceful arm and hand movements, her expressive face, her beautiful body's responses to the music?"

That evening, Lena asked her mirror if it could possibly be true, that she had agreed to devise a simple pantomime to accompany Theodore's rendition of "Clair de Lune." The reflected image nodded its head and slapped its cheeks.

Charles was enchanted in the evenings by his friends' rehearsal games, which consisted of Theodore seated on the little man's bed, humming and playing an imaginary piano, as Lena, much to her surprise, sometimes shed her self-consciousness and allowed the music to move into her hands and spine.

Since an actual performance was never mentioned, Lena came to believe that Theodore, too, considered all they were doing a charming game, and nothing more. She was not prepared for her colleague's reaction, following an especially lively experiment during which Charles clapped his hands and sang.

"This Thursday!" Theodore suddenly proclaimed. "Lena, keep everything you did tonight exactly the same." He grasped Lena's hand and squeezed it. "You, my dear, are about to make your comeback!"

Lena could tell that Theodore had been ready for an argument after making his pronouncement, and she had found unexpected pleasure in suppressing her urge to accommodate him. His eyes were as round as Charles's when she kissed each man on the forehead, then wheeled back to her room. Sitting alone on the edge of her bed, Lena reached for Myra's photograph.

"Well, my darling friend, do you believe it? Here I am about to become one of the dreaded Endless Re-runs we loved to poke fun at. No need to fret," she added, setting the silver frame back on her nightstand. "This will be a one-time comeback." She lay back on the pillow and continued the visit with Myra.

"I won't look any more foolish than Arnold playing his spoons, or Neva reciting Edgar Guest. Besides, Myra, what earthly reason is there for *not* doing it? The worst that can happen is they will laugh." Lena switched off the bed lamp and delivered her last sleepy thoughts to the darkness. "… and who am I to begrudge such a blessing to these people?"

Throughout Wednesday, Lena felt all of the old excitement

she recalled from the "Isadora Springtime." She sensed some of the shiniest threads from her youth being pulled into a good, taut stretch. She decided to use the blue scarf for the performance, to place it over her face and trace her features with her fingers through the thin fabric. This would create the "mysterious" section of the music. "Clair de Lune" shimmered in her inner ears the entire day. To end the evening, she read Emily Dickinson poems to Charles. The words meant little to him, but their sound made him happy. The lines calmed Lena and made the idea of going to bed seem possible.

Theodore oversaw the final arrangements in the recreation hall on Thursday afternoon. Miss Wilson was the only staff member let in on the coming surprise. Both Lena and Theodore were amazed by the enthusiasm with which the nurse played her part as co-conspirator. With slipping shoes and many grunts, she managed to push the upright piano to the left of center stage. She even had the receptionist fashion an amber gel from the plastic wrapping on a fruit basket. Theodore thanked Miss Wilson for her help, underscoring his gratitude with flashy glissandos on the keyboard, then wheeled back to his room for a light supper and a change into the old blue-and-white blazer from his dance band days.

Picturing himself as Nelson Eddy, about to sweep Jeanette MacDonald off her feet, Theodore waltzed his wheelchair down the corridor. Outside Lena's room, he crooned, "When I'm calling yoo-oo-oo-oo," pushed past the doorway, and pivoted to face her on the final "ooo." Lena was sitting next to her bed with the dinner tray on her lap.

"Dining at this hour?" Theodore teased. "How fashionable!"

Lena didn't answer. She stared at her tray.

"But, my dear Jeanette... Well, what on earth is wrong with me? You aren't Miss MacDonald. It's the elegant Miss Isadora, if I'm not mistaken."

Lena still didn't answer. Realizing stage fright had its nasty claws into her, Theodore moved his chair close enough to lay a hand on her shoulder.

"Just relax, Lena. Eat a bite and then we'll have a few minutes of fun in the spotlight. Only that," he added, patting her arm, "...

a little bit of fun."

"But Theodore, I can't."

"I know — I've felt that way plenty of times. Just take a spoonful of applesauce for good luck. You'll feel better."

"But... which is it?" Lena asked, looking straight into his eyes.

"The apple sauce? Why it's that lovely yellow mushy stuff in the pink bowl."

"Lena stared at her partner's pointing finger. "I mean the spoon," she said. "Is *that* the spoon, Theodore? I can't seem to figure it out."

South Beulah, Minnesota — Harold Huber

Blood Brothers

1937

If you step on a nail, the first thing you do is pull it out. The second is you stick it through something red and hang it high above your head when you go to bed. Then you don't get blood poison. I learned that from Mr. Rags way back when me and him were best friends. How I met him was I always had a stand in the back alley. A stand is a kind of store. I had my own business at the age of nine years old. I sold used comic books, used toys, used marbles and pollywogs. These are sometimes called tadpoles. I had the most customers for pollywogs, and second was comic books. I got the pollywogs at the dump a block from my house. I could find hundreds of them—usually in empty coffee cans full of water, but sometimes in parts of barrels and wagons that didn't leak.

The water has to be very old and then the pollywogs will be there. Mr. Rags told me they would not turn into frogs but to mosquitoes. So I put that on my sign and sold five jars in one day. Mr. Rags was my sign-helper. I made the "TODDS STORE" and he drew two flowers.

I call him Mr. Rags, but all the other people called him plain Rags. That is because he bought your rags. He had a wooden cart painted black, and he pulled it by two poles that stuck out in front. He called, "Rags! Rags!" as he walked down the alley, and sometimes people came out and gave him their old clothes or traded him for something on his cart. This is called barter. The first time Mr. Rags met me, he bartered me two oranges with all the rotten cut off for one Captain Marvel. I call him *Mister* because it means more respectful than just Rags. His real name is

Mr. Kalas, but I'm the only one he told that to. That's because we were best friends then.

One day he asked me if I wanted to go with him on his rounds. I said yes right away and did it almost every day after that. He helped me make the "Closed" sign for my stand. We always started behind the hotel where the alley is all in bricks. The back of the hotel has an iron stairs that goes right up to the top of the building, and you know you would vomit if you went up there. We called, "Rags!" over and over, but lots of times nobody had any. Then came the IGA, and we always got oranges there from the big iron box... sometimes even watermelon. He cut off the rotten parts with a long knife with a white handle and all jewels covering it. It came from The Old Country. That's where Mr. Rags came from, too, and it must be *very* old because *he* is over one hundred years old. They did not have electric light bulbs or even a radio there.

He always bartered me for comic books. This is what he liked to give to his son, Nikos. Nikos couldn't come ragging with his father because he was very sick and very different. I asked Mr. Rags every time *how* he was different, but he didn't want to tell me. He said it made his heart hurt to talk about it. So I just saved my best comics for Nikos and stopped asking. All my comics came from the dump, and we went there every day. Anyone would be surprised to see how many good rags and comics you can find there for free at the dump. But you have to be careful when you do it. There are bums there and people that are called hoodlums. One time Mr. Rags saved us from them by hollering loud in his language from The Old Country, and then by making his fists smoke in their faces. The hoodlums got so scared when they saw his hands smoking, that they ran away and we were saved.

One other time at the dump, he threw me under the rags on his cart when a drunk man waved a gun at us. The drunk man was standing on top of a broken car without any doors. He was doing number-one when he saw us. He started to yell that me and Mr. Rags should repent our sins and go to Hell. He said he was sent to smite us down because we were Babylons. Mr. Rags quick pushed me on the cart and covered me up with a white wedding dress. I heard him say the words again. Then I heard the

Blood Brothers

drunk man make a croaky sound and lots of racket and then nothing. When I came out from under everything, I couldn't see the man anywhere. I even looked inside the car and under the hood. Mr. Rags laughed and mussed up my hair and told me not to ask so many questions.

My friend taught me the best tricks there are. If I wanted to be, I could be the greatest magician in the world. But I am not to do any of the tricks where other people can see me. I will be struck dead if I do. He said they are secret tricks and you only must do them with your blood brothers. How we are blood brothers is that he had a very big blue jewel like a diamond with a pin to stick it into your clothes. First we went to the place in the dump where the cliff-swallows make their holes. We squatted down there and Mr. Rags held the jewel tight in his fist until it got warm from the blood under his skin. When he opened his fingers, the jewel was all wet and it sparkled. He told me a word to say so the pin prick wouldn't hurt… and it didn't! Then we pressed our wrists together and the blood made us blood brothers. Now our spirits will ever be together.

I loved Mr. Rags when we were best friends. I wished he could be my father instead of my real one. Mr. Rags always patted my neck and said I was his other son. One day I patted my real father's neck. I thought it would make him like me more. But that was on a drunk day, so it didn't work. Even my mother has to be careful when he's drunk. She liked it when I patted *her* neck, but the trouble with my mother is you must make sure she doesn't have her nervous headaches. I think she had one the day I patted her, because she cried while she said to clean up my mess in the alley. Mr. Rags *never* gets mad and he thinks being drunk is the wrong thing—like that man in the dump. He doesn't believe in headaches or that messes hurt you. Some day Mr. Rags will take me to live with him is what he promised me. Then I will be very happy.

I saved a good comic for Nikos every time I had my stand. I tried to give them as a present for Nikos, but Mr. Rags said we had to barter. He usually bartered me fruit and sometimes a smashed cake with still plenty of frosting left. The best was when he bartered me new tricks, but he was nervous that I would do them for other people. I had to prick open my brother-spot to

South Beulah, Minnesota   Harold Huber

make sure he believed me that I wouldn't. It made me feel so good when he told me that Nikos loved the comics I saved for him. I thought it must be awful not to go ragging with his father, and maybe the comics made up for it.

When my birthday was coming the next day, Mr. Rags asked me what I wanted for a present. I said it was something he *could* give me, but I knew he wouldn't want to. He promised that if it was something he could give, he would do it. I made him touch blood-spots and then I told him. I said I wanted to meet Nikos. Mr. Rags didn't say anything for a very long time. He kept turning his big ring around and around on his finger. Then he patted my neck and said, OKAY Little Toad—that was how it sounded when he meant "Little Todd"—he would bring his son the next day.

When I got to the dump, I thought Mr. Rags broke his promise. No one was with him... only his cart full of rags. His eyes looked funny when he said Happy Birthday. When I asked him where's Nikos, he moved his head for me to follow him to the cliff-swallow place where it's very private. The cliffs are at the back of the dump where nothing good is and nobody goes. When we got there, he put his hands on my cheeks and said he didn't forget his promise. I had to stand right up between the cart handles and then he threw back a lumpy piece of cloth. All I could see was the top thing of a baby buggy like a curved roof. Mr. Rags put his arm around my shoulder and then folded the buggy roof back.

There was Nikos. He didn't have any clothes on and all around him was black velvet like when you buy a diamond ring. His skin was white like a grub worm and he didn't have any arms. He was littler than me, but his head was bigger than Mr. Rags' and he couldn't lift it off the velvet. I thought I was going to have to be sick, but I didn't so that I wouldn't hurt Mr. Rags' feelings. I held out an almost new Rin Tin Tin and laid it on his stomach. I told him, "This is for you, Nikos... a present on my birthday." His eyes rolled down slow until they could see the comic and then his mouth laughed. When he started to grunt, Mr. Rags said I should put my wrist on his mouth. He sucked on my arm and then started to cry. Mr. Rags pulled down the buggy roof and patted my neck. He was crying, too. When a hundred year old man is crying, it makes you feel very sad. Then he pushed the cart down the alley and went home.

My father didn't like it when he found out that I went with Mr. Rags. My father said he was a black jew and a gypsy. He hated Mr. Rags and he didn't even know him! My mother cried so hard to me that I had to cry, too. When she was hugging me, that's when I thought I could trust her. I told her about the poor little boy with no arms so she would feel sorry and let me stay friends with Mr. Rags. That was the worst mistake that could ever be. She told my father and he started calling people on the telephone. I screamed at him that he should leave Mr. Rags alone. I never saw him get so mad. He made my nose bleed and locked me in my room. I hate him for what he did. I even hate my mother, too. She is a Babylon.

Mr. Rags has not been in the alley since my birthday. My mother and father say I must never speak his name again, but I speak it all the time... to myself. His picture was in the papers. It said he lived in the back of the caves where the IGA grows mushrooms, and that he is accused of insanity. They found Mrs. Rags there, too. Mrs. T. Kalas. She was a modern Egyptian mummy. They also accuse him of murder, but Mr. Rags said nobody killed her. She just died. I believe him. I know it's true. They made him go to a place called Black Falls. The papers did not talk about Nikos at all. Even when grown-ups talk to my parents, they never say Nikos. Nobody found him there. Nobody believes he *is*... except me. I tried to think of how to go to the caves and find Nikos and take care of him.

My father and mother said when I start school, this nonsense will go out of my head. That's what they called him... "nonsense." It means something to laugh at! They are wrong though. Nothing is going out of my head. They won't laugh pretty soon.

At night I practice the tricks Mr. Rags taught me... I mean only the one trick. When my father and mother are asleep, I take off my pajamas and go to the mirror in my room. I can see it even when the lights are out. I squeeze my hands together so hard that they shake. I make my eyes go cross-eyed and stick my tongue out as far as it will go. Then I push my chin down on my neck

South Beulah, Minnesota   Harold Huber

until it feels like I will blow up. As soon as I can make my hands smoke, then it is time. I will put my hands against the mirror on each side of my face. The glass will turn red and there will be Mr. Rags! Nikos will be sitting on his shoulders and he will be all well. His mouth will be open and laughing again. When they talk to me in Mr. Rag's old language, I will understand what they are saying. They will break through the glass and take me with them and teach me to talk the pretty words they say. Our spirits will ever be together... that is what my blood brother told me. I believe him. I know it is true. I will be happy living somewhere else.

Polly's Dance

1940

When the newspapers came in, Marliss read the article out loud before she let any of the customers buy their own copies. Then, while they stood right there in the aisles and read it again for themselves, Marliss made her big announcement.

"Polly Vik is now a Beulah Lake legend!"

What Marliss says is wrong. Even if I am still a kid, I know that much.

No one in this town understands a thing that's real about Polly, so how can she be their legend? Besides, there's got to be a picture.

A clear, shining, none-other-like-it picture has to shoot into your mind whenever you think of someone legendary — just hear their name. George Washington standing in that boat, Joan of Arc tied to a stake, like that. People here read the words and talk a lot, but they don't *see* anything. It's different for me. I see what happened out on the lake. I see what's real. Polly is my very own private and true legend.

* * *

Roman Vik and his wife, Polly, moved here from somewhere down south. Illinois or one of those places. It was three years ago, when I was twelve. They set up a little Gift Shop in the added-on part of Marliss's store. Polly made pictures to sell, smaller than postcards. Baby gophers and birds and cottontails and what-all. I bought one with my fifteen cents from bike-delivering groceries. It was of a killdeer in boots, with pinch-glasses on, and a cigarette holder in its beak. It was supposed to make you think of the old president, Franklin D. Roosevelt.

Mr. Vik sold stones. You should have seen those stones! They came in more colors than rainbows do, and some had gold in them. There was this one I wanted hard, but it cost five dollars. I figured that meant Mr. Vik didn't really want to sell it. It was split in half and each side had a cave in the middle where pink and yellow diamonds clung on the edges like chiseled-down icicles. I looked at that stone every day, but never let myself even touch it. Didn't dare to. They sold other things in the shop, too. Antiques, I guess. Old stuff they brought with from Illinois.

Nobody could understand how they earned enough money to buy even that bitty piece of land at the marshy end of the lake, but they bought it and Mr. Vik built a small house on it. The man from the lumber yard said the wood and nails got paid for with gold dollars, out of a box painted all over with squirrels. After the news about the gold dollars got out, everybody in Beulah Lake was suddenly very interested in the Viks.

I never saw Mr. Vik go hunting, but I saw him go fishing lots of times, even through the ice in winter. I guess fish is mostly what they ate. Anyway, he took that heavy old boat out every day he could. But there's one thing about Beulah Lake. She makes her own strip of weather over the water, separate from what it's like in town. She can whip up a wind out there when nobody expects it, and when she does, Beulah's as mean as two oceans. That's what happened one spring morning, and nobody ever saw Mr. Vik again.

Two days later, when the wind finally let off, a friend of Marliss's towed the boat to Polly's bit of shoreline. He found it floating empty over near where the river comes in. I was on the bridge and saw him find the boat. As soon as I realized where he was heading, I aimed my bike to the same place. When I turned in the Vik's road, the man had just thrown the anchor in the sand and was knocking on Polly's door.

All the time he talked to her, Polly never moved. She still stood in the doorway a long time after the man rowed away. Finally, she pulled the door closed behind her and walked down to the beached boat. She sat on a stump and just stared straight ahead. I

Polly's Dance

thought I should do something — go to her and say something — but what would I say or do? After a while, I walked as quiet as I could and sat on another stump a little ways behind her. She twisted to look at me, then turned her face back to the boat to stare some more. I felt so bad for her that I cried into my knees, even if I was a big teenager. That's when it came to me that I had to be her friend. *Had* to be, like it was one of the Ten Commandments or something. The problem was, how do you be a friend to someone who is as old as your grandma?

Right after school Monday, I biked back to the cottage with a present. I saved out one cupcake and half a sandwich from my lunch, and put it in a white box I found. I put a note in alongside. "I am so sorry for you, Mrs. Vik. Yours truly, Daniel Bleeder." She was by the boat when I pulled up and handed her the box. After she looked at the present and read my note, she took both my hands and squeezed them. She didn't let go for the longest time. When she did, she told me I should call her Polly. That hand-squeeze was the first minute of our friendship, and now — today — I say it was the first brush stroke.

* * *

Later that summer, Polly called from inside the cottage that I should please wait and help her with something. Funny, how she'd talk from inside to me outside, and only that one time ask me to come in. Anyway, this day she came out in a straw hat and apron, holding an old-time casting rod. I should please help her push the boat from up on the sand down to the water. I asked was she aiming to go fishing, and said I never saw her out in the boat with Mr. Vik. She answered, yes, that ghosts of fresh perch were haunting her taste buds and, no, she'd never fished before — but she was doing it now! I offered to go with and show her a few tricks, but she only wanted help launching the boat. I should run on home — didn't know when she would get back.

You can bet I didn't run on home. I sat on the sand and watched her change over from awkward slaps with the oars to smooth-as-silk gliding in hardly no time at all. Polly didn't stop rowing until all I could make out was a speck of a boat with a bump sticking up from it. The bump moved back and forth, but I couldn't tell what was exactly happening. The next day, after school, I told her she sure learned how to row fast. Her answer was a real "Polly Answer." She said, "Why learn *slow*?" I asked did she catch any perch. "Maybe," she said, then bent down to pick more potato bugs, so I didn't ask my other questions.

Every morning afterwards, unless the waves were high or the lake was iced over, Polly took that boat through the water and did whatever she did out there.

I knew fishing wasn't the main thing, but that's all I knew... except the boat always looked to be in the same spot when she'd stop rowing. I bet you can imagine how the town was buzzing. Not only was she parked every day on the lake, in a spot where no fish alive would be, she also closed up the shop at Marliss's for good, then moved everything into her peanut of a house.

It wasn't long before the few who once in awhile looked in on Polly stopped doing it. Too odd, too clammed up. Not nearly grateful enough for their visits. Too stuck up and proud, too blamed independent. They quit going to see Polly, but they kept good track of her. On some days, if the sun was just right, it looked like lots of flashbulbs going off, there were that many binoculars bobbing around. The same unsatisfying reports got passed around at Marliss's over and over. For a couple weeks, I got the third degree every time I went in the store. Finally, people realized I wasn't going to give them the scoop on what Polly did out there in the middle of the lake. I couldn't have if I'd wanted to—but they thought I was being stubborn.

***

It happened this way—the day Polly invited me inside the cottage. The October after we became friends, Beulah River was thick with tullibees going upstream to spawn. I kept one big beauty alive in a wagon full of water and showed Polly. My thought was right, she'd never seen the likes of a tullibee before. Talk about excited! She said the scales were made out of mirror, that the whole fish was purest silver with onyx nickels for eyes. Could she please keep the tullibee? Maybe try a painting of it?

Polly's Dance

When I said that's why I brought it, that's when she invited me to come inside. I should have a seat and make myself to home.

Everything from the Gift Shop was in boxes, set in rows along the baseboards.

Some of the beautiful rocks were arranged along window sills, including my special favorite with the diamond caves. Polly's tiny paintings covered the walls. My eyes were so filled up with wonderful sights that I didn't even bother to hate the "silver tea" she served—hot water with milk and sugar in it.

Polly asked me lots of questions that day. Mostly she wanted to make sure my parents knew about our friendship. When I told her that my mother and father were what is called "bohemians," she looked real surprised. I thought for sure Marliss would have told her before. She tells everybody *that*. When I said they liked it that my new friend was an artist, Polly pushed me on the shoulder and looked happy. Then she really started telling me all about herself. She even answered the one question I never would have the nerve to ask—how she and Mr. Vik lived without earning hardly any money.

"Roman found a picture one time," she said. A rich man in Chicago gave them a "sin full" of money for it, half in gold coins. She told me there was still enough for her to get by on, but only a few gold pieces were left.

We ended up looking at a poster pinned near the door. It showed a map of Beulah Lake, the kind with squiggly lines to tell you how deep the water is at different spots. Polly pointed to where the lines tightened in like a bull's eye and showed the deepest hole in the lake. If I imagined looking at the map sideways, then I would see that it was shaped like a funnel. "A funnel one-hundred and twenty feet down!" she said. Her finger stayed on that spot a long time while she looked, but she didn't say a word. Finally she whispered to me, "There's where Roman is."

The way she figured, that deepest hole was a *real* funnel, and that the lake water ran out of a little opening at the tip, down into the middle of the earth. Her idea was that the old water had to go *someplace*, so there would be room for new rain and winter melts. The pull of the draining water moved everything on the bottom slowly, slowly to that deepest spot. She knew by that time her

Roman was there, curled around the tip, resting… waiting.

I felt very nervous because I was sure she was going to tell me about her trips out on the lake. Instead, she brought more silver tea and put out a dish of pickled mushroom. Then, just when I thought our talk was over, she spilled the beans! She never did go fishing at all—all those long rows across the water. She acted-out each thing as she told me.

Every morning, Polly chose something she knew her husband loved—a chunk of crystals, one of her animal pictures, maybe a book or clay flower—and tied it to the loose end of the fishline. Then she rubbed above the knot with a dull kitchen knife until the line was thin and weak. She always tested to make sure it could just bear the weight of whatever she attached that day.

She would row in a straight line south, like it showed on the map, until, like on the map too, Beck's Peninsula was over her left shoulder and the bridge at Beulah River was over the other. That's when she knew the boat was right above the funnel. She said she also knew it because of a feeling that moved into the middle of her. The anchor rope was way too short to touch bottom there, so she sometimes had to work the oars to stay where she wanted.

* * *

I just about had to give up delivering groceries for Marliss. It must have showed in my eyes some way, that I knew what Polly was up to on the lake. The regulars there would try to get me off alone, then pump questions at me with both barrels. I tried not to look them in the eyes. I had the feeling that the pictures I had been making stronger and stronger in my mind might show.

Polly standing up in the boat. Her arm making slow sweeps from one side to the other. Gold coins glittering out of her hand in long curves into the water, the way sowing grain used to be done in olden days. Polly letting out line while Roman's gift sinks to the deep hole. The line going limp when it hits bottom. Polly sitting down, tightening and straightening the line. Polly being connected again to the person she loves. Then her lips push together and she snaps the pole upward to break the line.

Polly's Dance

Those first nights in bed, after Polly told me everything, I don't guess I hardly slept at all. I kept thinking of how hard it must have been, her being an old lady, rowing so far day after day, doing all that she did out there. Pretty soon I could see all the scenes as clear as if I had watched every bit myself, above the water and under. That's why I had to be so careful when I looked at those nosey customers at the store.

Now I'll tell the last part.

* * *

I caught two big walleyes at the bridge one afternoon, so I cleaned them and brought them to Polly. She was so happy to have fresh fish and, as usual, made a big deal out of what nice fillets I cut and how she wished there was some wonderful way to repay me. I didn't mean anything by it, but right when she said that about how I should be paid, she saw me looking at the beautiful "diamond" rock I always loved. Before she could do or say anything, I put on a big show of being insulted. "I don't charge my friends when I bring them presents," is what I said. She caught on that it was a joke, and we both got to laughing hard. The laugh choked in my throat when I realized what Polly was doing all the while we were talking.

The rope was about ten feet long. It looked like it was cut off from the boat's anchor. Polly had tied one end in a slip-knot and was winding the rest into a loose coil. I made myself calm down before I talked.

"You going to drop some guy off a scaffold?" I asked her.

"Oh no!" she laughed — a real jolly laugh, so I felt a little better.

"And it's not to wrap around a lady's neck, either?" I tried to pretend I was making sport, but it came out sounding stupid.

"No-o-o!" This time, it was a tickled-pink laugh. "… just the opposite."

Well, she was getting such a kick out of my questions, that I ended up sighing a big sigh of relief.

Polly thanked me again for the walleyes, and I headed for my bike. Before leaving, I reminded her that it wouldn't be long until the first frost set in and that I'd help beach the boat and flip it over, so the snow could make it a whale belly again, like last winter. This time when she laughed, she really did look like the pretty young girl she must have been when her and Mr. Vik were meeting and flirting and learning how to love each other.

The blinds were down and the boat was gone when I got there at seven the next morning. Polly never went out on the lake that early before, so I didn't know what to think. I biked back in the afternoon, but she wasn't there. I tried again that night. Same thing. I got sick to my stomach.

One shoulder-push is all it took to force the door. Polly wasn't there. Neither was all the stuff from the Gift Shop that had lined the walls, except... Setting on the kitchen table, on a fancy old doily, snapping the beam from my flashlight into a hundred splinters, was the split-open rock. I knew the little caves with their diamonds were mine now. I knew I would never see my friend again.

The article in *South Beulah Weekly* was so awful. I'm glad I didn't read it in the store, with everyone watching. It started out, "BEULAH RECLUSE MISSING — PRESUMED DROWNED," then came a dozen gray lines — facts. Everything about them was wrong. Not one single word that was important or truthful about Polly. Cold-blooded lines that didn't add up to anything.

If the newspaper had asked me to write about Polly, I would have tried to make a poem or a song. I would have used the finest words I know and turned them into a scene:

> *There is a reunion party tonight in Beulah Lake, at one hundred and twenty feet. Polly Vik is dancing for her husband. Roman Vik is spiffed up in his whitest bones. He is laying on his back with both hands tucked behind his head. His sandy couch is covered with gold coins and treasure of every kind.*
>
> *Polly's dance is a slow spinning one. She turns and turns, graceful and dainty. A yellow braid-line makes a bracelet for her ankles, and her arms and apron swell out full as she spins around. Her gray hair is loose and floats upward.*
>
> *The lights are low, down there on Polly and Roman, but tullibees dart around them, making green and silver glints to*

Polly's Dance

mix with the wavery patches of light from high above. The smiling couple and the tullibees hear waltzes in the waves.

Well, the paper would never print such words. They'd want to send a reporter—maybe Marliss—down under the water to check out the facts, only they wouldn't find any. My report would be art, and real art isn't about facts. It's beautiful made-up lies that stand for what is true.

Polly told me that turning someone you love into a work of art lets that person live forever. She said it gives them a place to be... to come back to. That's why I painted Polly's dance for myself and hung it in my mind. Whenever I need to, I close my eyes and look at the picture. Polly is alive there—alongside her Roman again—smiling in the new world I made up for her—winking at me and laughing at me for calling her a legend. Afterwards, I can even be nice to Marliss... for a while.

South Beulah, Minnesota   Harold Huber

Letter To Charles

1999

Dear Charles,
    This here's a double barrel shock for you. Me writing a letter. Your ma always did the letter writing, and since she passed on I ain't ever had the urge. But now today I got to write you one. The other barrel is that I'm telling you I don't like you anymore. What you said yesterday when you drove away hurt me deep. What kind of a person has that big company turned you into anyway? Here's what I'm getting at. You don't owe me one, like you said. I never thought...

Dear Gabriel,
    Do you remember me? It's Billy, your old ten-year-old pal you used to raise hell with in every cranny of South Beulah. I don't know what come over me today but I got a letter writing bug and you're who I thought of. I ain't wrote a letter in sixty years. I tried writing one to my boy Charles, but it didn't work out good. So I'm practicing on you, Gabe.
    Wish I wrote you sixty years ago when I moved here. Then you would of wrote back and we would know how life went for each other. Did you know you was my hero, like they say, when we was growing up together? Well you was. Maybe because you was over thirteen when I was only ten. Anyways, I learned half my thoughts from you.
    Remember that winter when me and you drove the haywagon across all those miles of field to Ma and Pa's house they was to

move into? Remember how cold that ride got and how deep the snow was? I hardly thought we'd make it most of the trip. A wonder poor Whiskey didn't freeze to his iron shoes. Guess the horse blanket saved him.

We was supposed to unload stuff into the house so that would be done when the folks came in the morning. I guess they never gave it a passing about the house being cold as outside. With us with no wood or nothing for the heat stove. And no food except the big milk can full of froze milk by the time we got there. Nothing ever tasted so good since, as that froze cream on the top. That's one of the things you learned me. That is still my favorite treat, only now it comes in cartons and I put sugar on it.

We'd of been goners that night if you didn't think of Whiskey's blanket. He looked big as a elephant in that empty parlor, didn't he? Just me and you and the bunch of chairs we hauled. Then the three of us snuggled under that itchy cover is what saved our lives I know. See why you was my hero?

I wish I could of saved your life Gabe. Some folks from Beulah came up to Emily's funeral and they told me about you dying from a heart attack. It made me feel twice as blue as I was already. Boy, I wish I would of wrote you lots of letters before that happened. That would of made me feel like I thanked you some for all the good times you made happen.

Well this sure is a long letter. Wish you could read it. Now my motor is going so I'll try one to Charles again. Your friend, Bill.

Dear Charles,

I hope you made it back to St. Paul okay. I hope you didn't talk so much on that telephone in your car that you forgot to pay attention to the road. Are you surprised to get a letter from your old father? I was never much good at letters, but I want to write you some things about yesterday.

Charles, I didn't like it, what you said when you left here. That about *owing me one*. It was almost as bad as you giving Eugene a hundred dollar bill for fixing your car hood. Both things was all wrong, don't you know that? A favor ain't the same thing as getting a loan, with bookkeeping like business, you owe me for this then I'll owe you for that. A favor is something you do for

Letter To Charles

a present to somebody. It's what you want to do, with no strings. I got that hundred dollars here for you next time you come back.
Charles, how could you forget all what your ma and me...

Dear Gabriel,
I'm back to you again. Sorry, but I know you won't complain. I tried writing my boy again but it kept coming out hateful. I think it will help to palaver with you a while. That first letter came out so easy, maybe I'll catch the hang of it. Letter writing.
I bet you grew up to be a nice man Gabe. Even tho you was as much a heller as me, my sister Willie always said you had meat in your brains and that you would turn out fine, and that's what I thought, too. I wonder if you met a beautiful girl and got married. If you did, I hope she was half as fine as my Emily. And did you have a flock of kids, too, that's what I wonder. And are they alive now, and is your lady, too? They will be carrying around a load of memories of you, so you ain't dead in that way.
Too bad they wasn't with on our Whiskey trip that winter. But then they got their own good stories to think back on. I bet your kids went to college, too, like my Charles. They all seem to do that these days. Trouble with college is it kinda makes them from a different country or something. Their talk gets hard to understand and some of the ways they think and treat you.
My boy was here yesterday for the day, but I didn't see much of him even tho it was almost a year since last time he came. Some men from a company in town came and picked him up for a meeting. It has to be that way I guess when you are a big gun in a business. Computers and all stuff like that. A mystery to me.
Anyways, Charlie left his car here. You should see that car! It is little and bright red and only fits two people, but it cost enough to buy a house. The sun dawns and sets on that car, as they say, and he was upset because hail made a big dent in the hood. I went to surprise him by asking my friend Eugene to come over and take a look. Eugene can talk to steel with his hammer and mallet sweet as you'd talk to a lover. When Charles got back, there wasn't a sign of no dent anywhere. Then my son did a thing that made me want to break down and cry.
He pulled out his wallet and gave Eugene a hundred dollar

bill! He didn't even say thank you to Eugene. He climbed in the car and talked to me thru the window. It rolled down without Charles even touching it. He couldn't stay to visit. Another meeting in one hour. When he started pulling away, he leaned out and said *I owe you one, Dad.* Isn't that a shameful sin Gabe?

Did your kids call you Dad? I don't know, I don't much like it. You hear it all the time nowadays. Maybe it comes from college. We always said Ma and Pa to our folks. Seems more natural sounding. Seems like there's more love caught in those bitty words. Well that ain't what I want to write you about. It's that about the money and that owing me one.

I don't know why it got to me so bad. Am I crazy Gabe? Isn't it all wrong? I don't know, maybe Emily should of let me spank him those coupla times. Maybe I just messed up on being a good father to him. Maybe Willie told me stuff like all this and I forgot. Wish you could write me a letter and tell me what you think.

Remember Willie? She was mother to me as well as being my big sister. Did you realize that? I didn't really until I got older. She thought you were the cat's pajamas and she liked it that we played together. I know I could write about this owe-you thing to Willie but... Well to tell the truth, I'm ashamed to write her. She's been at Memorial Home over a year and I only went to see her once in all that time. I've been blaming it on me never learning to drive.

Anyways now I'm ashamed to face her even in a letter. I should...

Dear Charlie,

Seems like a year gone by since you was here yesterday. Can you believe you are reading a letter from your father? I can't hardly either. It's that there's something I got to get off my chest. So that's why this letter out of the clear blue with all the no schooling showing. I hope you can read the sense of it.

Charlie I got to tell you I got plenty mad the way you said to me *I owe you one.* Almost even worst was you giving Eugene that money. Charlie, you didn't owe for that dent or for me getting Eugene to fix it. We cooked it up between us to be a surprise for you. Like for a birthday present even if yours ain't until March. Then you bring out money, and so much! And you say you owe

Letter To Charles

me on top of it. Our feelings was both hurt. Couldn't you see that...

Dear Gabe,

I never thought I believed in ghosts but now I guess I got to. You're one, ain't you? You always used to steer me right when we was little and now you're doing it again. I suppose you ain't allowed to talk to me straight out, but leave it to you to find a way anyways.

I got so flustered trying to get that letter wrote to my boy I had to lay down for a nap. That's when you did it, didn't you? Before I knew I was asleep there you was outside the machine shed. Your overalls was ripped in the knees like usual. You said *stand right there Billy*. And when I started running you tackled me flat and almost crunched my privates sitting on my belly. You did the same old thing — pin my arms above my head and sink your eyes right into me. I don't think you said anything then, but I got the message right enough. Your eyes was hollering louder than ten voice boxes.

Not knowing how to drive was nothing but a truck load of horse apples, right? I was a coward about Willie, and I am just keeping on being a coward, right? Oh Gabe, you sure hit it on the head with that one.

What's there to stop me from taking a bus to where Willie is? It can't cost all that much. I ain't a starving gypsy, am I? So that's what I'm going to do, Gabe. On Monday I'll ask my friend to drive me to town and I'll get the Greyhound. I won't write Willie first. I'll just go there and hope I don't give her no screaming fit from the shock.

I don't want it to be like it was with you. Not thanking her decent for all she did. For seeing to me like her own child when Ma died. For so many other things I couldn't all write down. I'll tell her how much in the world she means to me. I'll talk to her about you, too, Gabe. She'll like that. Maybe then she might forgive the way I been so selfish all this time. And maybe she can help me know what to do about Charles. I suppose I won't mention to her your being a ghost or nothing. Or maybe I will. I got a hunch she'd like knowing you're still hanging around.

South Beulah, Minnesota   Harold Huber

Oh boy, Gabe!, Now I'm so excited about getting on that bus. I'm just about higher than a kite. Won't she be glad to see me? Oh Gabriel—she *will* be glad, won't she? I didn't go and wait too long. I sure hope. No. Not unless Willie is changed into somebody else. She's more like to swat my butt and make me kiss her twice. *A just punishment* she'll say like she used to.

Thank you, Gabriel, for picking up where you left off at. Even if you ain't a real ghost, and I'm just imagining you, I'm taking you on as gospel. Gabe, ain't we all a bunch of fools? Us live ones?

I will be writing you letters regular from now on. I can tell there's something healthful in doing it. I will tell you about Willie on Tuesday.

Dear Son,

I'm taking up writing letters in my old age. Hope you can handle the shock. I loved it that you came to see me yesterday. I just wish our visit could have been longer.

I hope you got to your meeting on time and that you shined at it. After you went, Eugene asked me what your job was like. I was ashamed I didn't know much to tell him. The next time you come will you please tell me all about it and all what you do? I'm ready and itching to be proud of you.

Eugene says he won't take your money for fixing your dent. He says he wants it to be a present for the boy of his best friend. That's how Eugene is. I think it's a nice way to be. Anyways I have your hundred dollars here when you come.

Charlie, you said something to me that struck me odd, I owe you one Dad is what you said. Son you surely don't *owe* me for nothing. That owe is a hard word for me to use for somebody I love. And that there's the poop Charlie. I love you. I don't think I told you that lately, but you sure must know it's true. You owe *yourself* to be as good a man as you can be, but that's all the owing I can think of.

I expect you meant *return the favor* when you said that *owe*. There's an idea I truly like. Swapping favors is sheer fun as long as there's no one-for-one to it. You know—like it has to be in business. You can do me favors any old time you got a mind to, Charlie.

Letter To Charles

You got my full permission, I'll do the same. Is it a deal? I'll be seeing your Aunt Willie on Monday. Eugene's going to drive me to the bus depot so as I can get there. It's been too long since I seen her. Over a year. I bet she's the same bossy live wire as usual. That's what I'm hoping anyways. Remember what a funny take off she used to do on your ma? Remember how we'd laugh 'til we almost got sick—specially your ma? I bet that old gal would be tickled pink to see your wonderful new car some day. I know your work might make that a hard thing to do, but it's a possibility, as they say, right?

Here is a easier thing to think about. Now that I broke the ice and loaded up a envelope full of words to send you, maybe you could write me one, too. If you are anything like me, you'll find some fun in it. I'm starting to feel that you are a little bit like me but I don't want you to cry about that son. There is probably a pill you can take for it.

But would you do that sometime, Charlie? Write me a letter? I'd take it as a favor.

                        Your Pa